I0784306

DEDICATION

When Walls Talk

By Geralyn Hesslau Magrady

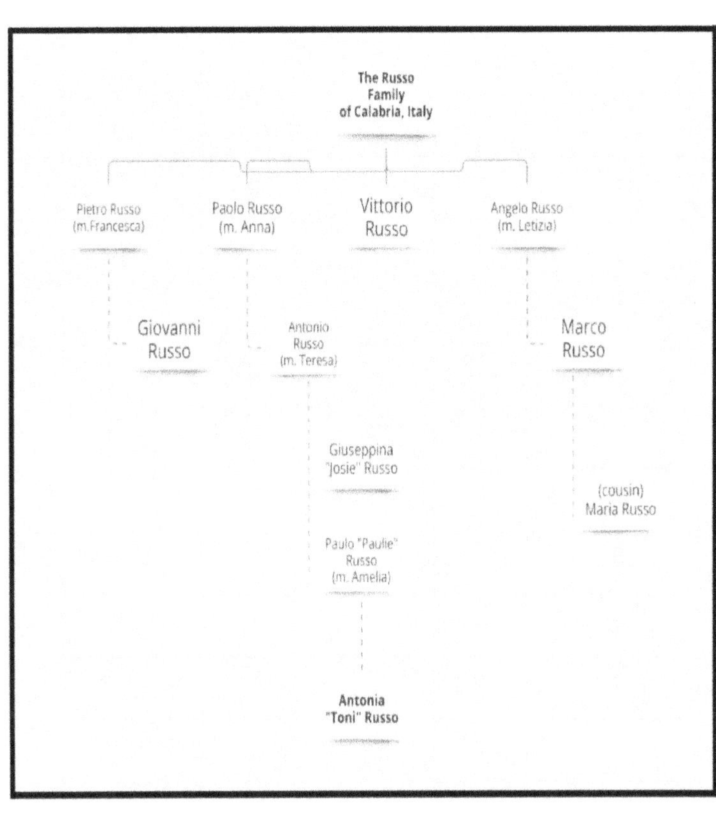

The Russo
Family
of Calabria, Italy
Pietro Russo
(m. Francesca)
Paolo Russo
(m. Anna)
Vittorio
Russo
Angelo Russo
(m. Letizia)
Giovanni
Russo
Antonio
Russo
(m. Teresa)
Marco
Russo
Giuseppina
"Josie" Russo
(cousin)
Maria Russo
Paulo "Paulie"
Russo
(m. Amelia)
Antonia
"Toni" Russo

Monday

Without knowing it was him, I knew it was him. Our eyes met as I walked through the door, and as I approached, I noticed his clean-shaven face and slight dimples. A boyish, wide smile beamed when he caught my eye.

"Toni?" he asked, standing with an outstretched right hand.

"The one and only," I said, receiving his handshake and feeling his left hand cover mine with a squeeze.

"Let me order you something. Coffee? Latte? Cappuccino?"

"Just a coffee. Thank you." *The one and only? Where did that come from, Toni?* "Black," I added.

He nodded, and when he walked toward the cashier, I tried not to watch his departure. *First impression. If he had gel in his hair, and if his eyes were a bit more pronounced, he would remind me of—Stop. Don't do that!*

I switched my focus to the coffee-themed café, the organic, brick walls offering juxtaposition to artwork that resembled pictures I'd seen in the home goods department at Kohls. Nothing too original here, but quaint nonetheless.

Surprisingly, conversation was easier than I had expected. He was good at getting me to expound on responses to open-ended questions without my feeling like I was being interviewed. I hadn't prepared a "get to know you" plan because I didn't figure on staying long, but I found myself enjoying his company. *How long has it been since I last told someone about me, about my teaching past and business future? When was the last time someone asked about my thoughts on classic vs. modern literature or the societal implications of technology?* Dialogue flowed between playful childhood memories and serious adult concerns.

"Do you believe in coincidence?" he asked.

The inquiry stumped me. I felt as if I'd heard the line a million times, but I couldn't recall my response. *If not coincidence, then what? Fate?* Once, in a book club, we discussed the themes of coincidence and determinism in *The Shadow of the Wind* by Carlos Ruiz Zafón. It was a lively talk, but I couldn't remember a definitive belief on my part. All I remembered was pondering examples of happenstance in other books like Dostoevsky's *Crime and Punishment,* Austen's *Pride and Prejudice,* Shakespeare's *Romeo and Juliet.* Maybe the common "coincidence" theme was what made me feel as if the question had been broached a million times, but in reality was simply a single, lingering thought. Kind-of like the magnolia tree. It wasn't that I'd seen a million magnolia trees, but I had studied the one that hung over my apartment balcony. It was my companion through countless pages of late night and early morning reports and lesson planning and grading, and because I understood its brief beauty, I could appreciate the blooming of all magnolias and wince at the thought of an eventual thunderstorm that would rip away its fragrant petals into a sludge of brown, coating the grass and walkway, a drudgery of clean up, while wet potpourri exacerbated the allergy season. I concluded a long time ago that life was like that magnolia: we shine, and then things out of our control will dim our brilliance, wreak havoc on our days; then we clean up and move on, keep living every day until we, like a newly blooming tree, get the opportunity to shine again.

"No," I replied confidently, as if I knew it to be true, as if all reality were fate, as if Vinny was supposed to die. But he *wasn't* supposed to die. *Was it fate or coincidence that a car pulled out at that precise time?*

The black coffee, now cooled, tasted more bitter than it had on my first sip.

"Actually, James. I don't know if I believe in coincidence." *And I'd rather not think about it.*

* * *

"So, talk to me. How was the date this morning?"

Claire always posed the big question as soon as we sat down. That was her M.O. since our first session when she opened with, "It's been a couple months since your husband's death. Where's your grief at?" Although the big question failed to startle me, it broke my shell wide open every time.

"It wasn't a date. I shouldn't have let my colleague—a *former* colleague—set this up."

"What happened?"

"He reminds me of Vinny. They have a lot in common."

"And that's bad?" she asked. "Can it be something good?"

"It's neither. I'm not ready."

"What aren't you ready for?"

I rolled my eyes. *She knows what I mean. Why make me say it?* "Two years is not enough time for me to move on." *Move on.* The words felt like betrayal, but for some reason, they didn't sound like one. "I'm not ready to let go, Claire."

"Moving on doesn't mean letting go, Toni. You'll forever embrace your past, but allowing yourself to embrace your present is okay, too."

I know. I know. But…

"They worked together. Years ago. They were cable guys at different shops for the same company. James worked cable while going to college; Vinny worked cable so that *I* could go to college." *Charles Darnay and Sydney Carton in a Tale of Two Cities. Did Dickens create their resemblance as a coincidence? An exaggeration, yes, but there* is *a likeness.*

"What does James do now?"

"He's a teacher," I confessed.

"So, you and James have something in common, too?"

"He teaches in the high school foreign language department." I was fishing for the right response, but nothing seemed right. "That's not the same as teaching middle school language arts."

Claire tilted her head and gave a slight smile. *She knows I'm fishing. A teacher is a teacher. It's the same.*

"We met for coffee. We didn't talk long. I didn't feel a connection." *Did I?* "I could only see Vinny's dark hair and dark eyes." I knew Claire was waiting for me to stop there. Even therapists, no matter their training, can't stifle their facial expression a hundred percent of the time. Her lips parted, ready for interjection, and then they relaxed, as if she caught herself.

"What?" I asked.

"How did things end?"

"He asked if he could take me out for dinner sometime."

"How did you respond?"

"I gave him my number and said maybe. He texted just as I arrived here, actually, to ask what I was doing on Thursday."

"How did you reply?"

"I wanted to see you before replying."

"You don't need anyone's approval, Toni."

* * *

When I got back to my car, I sighed. Vinny wanted me to be happy, but I had no idea how to be that anymore. *Who am I now? How do I find my new self?* I picked up my phone and typed a few lines.

"Hi James. This is Toni. Thursday sounds good."

I pressed "send." Within seconds, the ding sounded.

"Hi Toni! I'm glad you responded. I look forward to seeing you again."

* * *

I wasn't sure that going on a dinner date with James would be a good idea, but it was only Monday. I had time to back out. Cutting short my therapy session to make my noon meeting with the contractor, I had to switch gears from personal life to dream life.

The bookstore had been the imagination of my heart for decades. However, after all the hard work Vinny put forth to fund my education, I couldn't possibly move forward with anything but teaching. I loved teaching, truly, but I had to admit that I thought I'd have kids someday, maybe teach at my kids' school, maybe have the same days off for family time, maybe a summer vacation, maybe. But after years of trying and years of testing, it was determined that we couldn't. We were crushed. I assumed that the infertility was due to me; my mom had died of ovarian cancer when I was eighteen, and even though I had been closely monitored, it just seemed the most plausible that *I* was the reason. When Vinny was told he had varicoceles, we had no idea what that was. I assured Vinny over and over that our new reality didn't change my love and commitment to him nor to our marriage, that *"until death do us part"* was still as true on diagnosis day as the day we said "I do." *Irony, right?*

"We could adopt," I told my husband.

"Or we could *adapt*," Vinny said.

"What do you mean? Don't you want to have a family?"

If it hadn't been for the ticking of the kitchen clock, I would've thought we were frozen in time, just a snapshot on the refrigerator next to the reminder notes and recipe cards held steady by magnetic circles. With a quizzical expression, I tried to speak, but it might have shown confusion, sadness even. Vinny's expression, however, implored acceptance through a gentleness of soft eyes that begged for understanding, forgiveness.

"If I'm being honest, Toni, any children we adopt might be a constant reminder of what *I* couldn't give to you." Lines on his forehead formed as he lifted his brows. "I'm afraid I wouldn't be the father I'd want to be, and that wouldn't be fair to those kids." *No, Vinny! You would be a wonderful daddy to any child lucky enough to call you that!*

I held him, keeping my thoughts inside, while his arms tightened around me so hard that I could feel the quick pace of his heartbeat. Vinny had been thinking about his words. I had not.

He continued in a whisper, "Maybe we could adapt to being our own family, doing amazing things as a couple." His voice broke. "I still want to be the person who makes your dreams come true, Toni. Please let me do that."

"What are you thinking, Vinny?" I blurted. "You make dreams come true every day."

I was trying to form my words into a reassuring response when Vinny loosened his grip, stroked my arm, and pulled out a chair for me to sit down.

"Don't get mad," he started, holding my hands across the kitchen table. "I spoke with your dad, and he said he's been ready for years to let go of the family bakery." My mouth dropped, but he went on before I could retort. "Hell, Toni, it's not even a bakery anymore. He sells sandwiches and specialty cookies. But without you wanting to take it over, he was afraid he'd be disappointing your mother if he sold it to a stranger."

"I don't want to own a bakery or sandwich shop, Vinny. I made that clear a long time ago, and I doubt my mom would be disappointed in me following my own life path instead of my parents'."

"We could turn it into a bookstore, Toni."

My heart skipped a beat. *A bookstore?* For the first time in a year of let-downs and depression, the thought brought a grin to my face. On our first date, we had talked about dreams, and I told Vinny that I sometimes woke up in the middle of the night with thoughts of being in my own shop with author talks for adults, book clubs for teens, and storytimes for the little ones. It had been a while since we last talked about it, but he never forgot.

"It's been Russo Bakery for over eighty years," I reminded him.

"And it could be Russo Books for the next eighty."

"My dad agreed to this?"

"Your dad supports it wholeheartedly."

I'd have to quit teaching. We'd have to put our money into an endeavor that might not work out. It would be such a risk. Could I really commit to that kind of uncertainty? Could I leave education and start something new?

"You put me through college so I could be a teacher."

"With no regrets, Toni. When you were in your twenties, that's what your heart wanted. We change. We grow. Who knows what the future holds? But right now, the time is right for this. Schools will always be there." And that was true. I was almost thirty-two at the time. Still young enough to make a go of it. Still young enough to go back to teaching if I didn't become a new trendsetter for the local lit world. "It's your dream, Toni."

"But what about *your* dreams, Vinny? A bookstore is certainly not a Vinny Chiappeta dream."

"My only dream is the same one I've had since we started dating. To make you happy." He took my hands and kissed them. His sincerity and affection made me want to cry. "Please, Toni. Let's start this new adventure and see where it goes."

* * *

Just after signing the papers that made us the new owners of Russo Books, Vinny was in a motorcycle accident. Vinny was in a coma. Vinny was in post-coma unresponsiveness. Vinny died. Two years, two months, and eight days later, my dad set up a meeting with the contractor so that we could start the demo phase. "It's time," he told me. I agreed, but it felt more an obligation than a dream.

* * *

James, check. Claire, check. Richie, next. The day's schedule was on its way to completion, but every check mark thus far had been met with mixed emotions. The upcoming meeting would be no exception. I parked in front of the building on Taylor Street, not recalling the ride, the Ashland exit, the turns. *Did I even slow down at the red lights or stop signs?* It was as if my car simply knew how to navigate the city without a single thought from its driver. It was a natural destination; I had been driving this route for as long as I could remember. This time, however, was the first time I pulled up in front of the mocha-colored brick building without its awning and cinnamon-striped sign. All the physical blemishes shone: the caulk around the display window needed touch-ups, as did the chipped-away grout around the recessed doors; the entryway to the right that led to the upstairs apartment could use a new transom; the bakery entrance to the left looked surprisingly intact with the same wooden frame and thick, beveled glass. *It had to have been replaced at some point, right?* The glass sparkled, especially so with everything else entirely bare. I found myself staring at the large bay window, imagining all the little Russo children playing hopscotch and marbles on the sidewalk in front of it. The memory wasn't mine; it was my ancestors'. *Will they approve of the transformation? Could I bring back joy for them? For me?* A car drove past and snapped me from my trance. I grabbed my purse and notebook and whispered, "Here we go, Vinny. If I find happiness, your dream will come true." I got out, and before I stepped onto the curb, an airplane flew overhead, a common occurrence, but for some reason, I looked up at it, and with that I looked at the top of the building, at the terracotta blocks that lined the rooftop. *Why haven't I ever noticed those before?* I couldn't make out the decorative design, but what mattered most at the moment was the fact that they were there. Every building along the street had different terracotta blocks along its roofing, and I had never made the observation.

"C'mon, Toni. The contractor is waiting."

I waved at my dad who appeared in the doorway, and I walked in.

* * *

The shop looked twice the size without the counters and tables and chairs. Barren walls felt higher and wider without the family pictures and menu boards that had been packed away in the backyard shed. The kitchen behind the storefront was a clean slate. Dad had sold off the appliances and equipment.

"So, Paulie, the plan is to expand the front space into the old kitchen?"

"Right," Dad responded to the contractor. "Keep enough space in the back for an office, small bathroom, and storage room." He looked at me. "That's what you want, yes?"

I nodded.

Richie was middle-aged like my dad, and their fathers had been friends, as were their grandfathers. He was family because he grew up in the neighborhood, so when we needed a contractor to design a new floor plan to make this bookstore a reality, he was the first person Dad called. They had met over cappuccinos months prior, and the main concern back then was typical of any project with a structure built in the 1920s: the unknown. Old wiring and gas lines? Plumbing issues? There were always surprises when tearing down walls.

What made matters more puzzling were the missing blueprints. Although the bakery was built in the early 1920s, the only drawings dated to a renovation made in 1946. There should have been a post-WWI design, not just a post-WWII design. And interior measurements were off by at least three feet in the old kitchen. According to the 1946 plans, the span from the east wall to the west wall should have been twenty-five feet, but it measured less.

" 'Bout a three foot difference," Richie confirmed, as the metal strip of the tape measure retracted and made me jolt at the snap. "Too much coffee making you jumpy, Toni?"

I responded with a grin, and then Dad asked, "Everything on schedule for demo?"

Richie was in the process of knocking on all the plaster and drywall.

"Absolutely, boss." He continued his path around the shop walls. "Listen here," he said.

"What am I listening for?" Dad wondered.

"That hollow sound. Hear?" Richie knocked on two different walls to demonstrate the difference. "Must be an old pantry or closet that was closed up," the contractor concluded. "We'll find out more tomorrow."

I nodded again.

Richie probably expected a bit more enthusiasm on my part, but I didn't know how to reconnect the world around me with myself.

Claire had told me, "You'll forever embrace your past, but allowing yourself to embrace your present is okay, too." *But what if I didn't understand my past? Was my life with Vinny the only past I had?* No. This place had history, *my* history, and I needed to connect to it. *Why didn't I ever see the terracotta? What else has gone unnoticed, unasked? Just the way James and I were getting to know one another over coffee, I need to get to know myself.*

I couldn't believe I was thinking this way, but a little switch flipped inside me, and I didn't want to be detached anymore.

"I'd like to be here for the demo. I promise not to get in the way."

Richie smiled, and I smiled in return.

"I'll see you at 7am, Toni."

*   *   *

Dad ate dinner in the late afternoons, so once Richie had finished prepping downstairs, I joined my father in the apartment above, the place he returned home after the last of his ancestors passed away.

"I picked up some nduja from the deli down the street," he said, tearing the loaves of fresh Italian bread and spreading the spicy sausage on each piece. "Can you make a little Caprese salad for us?"

He pointed to the basket of garden tomatoes on the table and jars of basil on the window sill. I grabbed a ball of mozzarella from the fridge and cut the ingredients by his side.

"Is the deli still doing well?" I inquired as I sliced.

"The neighborhood has changed, Mimma, but loyalty thrives in Little Italy," he replied.

There was something nostalgic and endearing when he referred to me as "Mimma," and he used a hint of the Old World accent that had been lost through the generations.

"Tell me about the bakery, Dad—your experience here, why Mom was so dedicated as an in-law, more so than blood Russos." He heated a pan to fry an egg, his favorite way to top an nduja sandwich. "Why did Grandma and Grandpa move your family away when they still needed to commute to the shop?" I asked.

Dad set down two porcelain plates, probably the same dishes his grandparents used, the ones with little pink roses painted in the center. "Bring the salad," he requested. I placed the tomatoes and cheese and basil on each plate and drizzled the oil across the top, and after he served up the sandwiches, we sat. Like clockwork, my father bowed his head, and I copied his movement with folded hands. He mumbled a prayer of thanks, made the Sign of the Cross, and kissed the medallion around his neck.

"Why so many questions, Toni? Are you having second thoughts about the bookstore?"

He was right to wonder. Why the questions now? Why not when I was younger? I honestly didn't know why it seemed more important than ever to understand my family. All I knew was that I had never been so unsure of my present self, or my future self for that matter.

"Isn't this the age?" I responded after taking a first bite of the nduja. "A child is selfish and wants the family to take care of her. A teen is rebellious and wants family to stay away from her. A twenty-something thinks she knows it all and doesn't need family." A second bite of the nduja had me reaching for my glass of ice water.

It was an accurate summary of my life. As a child, I loved being my mother's sidekick when we went to the market or ran errands in the city because I was always rewarded with a treat or toy for good behavior, even if "good" was stretching it. After school, I tagged along back to the bakery, and after an hour being antsy and begging to go to the park, Auntie Josie used to tell my mom, "Go,

Amelia. Your baby wants some fresh air. Maria and I are fine on our own." And I picked my favorite ricotta cookies to bring with us as we headed down the street to throw a frisbee or ball, to play hide and seek or jump rope. We were buddies, and I couldn't recall a time when I didn't get my way. My mom was my best friend until sophomore year when I found new girlfriends at school and skipped family dinners to go to football games and movies and the mall. Then "the incident" happened. A friend and I told our parents we were spending the night at one another's house, but we actually went to a party and crashed there. When my friend pulled up to my home to drop me off, my mom was in the front window waiting, tears streaming down her face. I walked up the stairs and through the door, and she threw her arms around me. "Dear God, you're home safe." She pulled away and put her hands on my cheeks, rosary beads knotted through her fingers. "You said Shelly was spending the night at our house."

I was filled with anger. "No, Mom. I said I was staying at Shelly's."

"But you didn't. Where were you?" Her voice changed from relief to disappointment.

"Shelly's," I lied.

"When you didn't come home, I called Shelly's house, and neither of you were there. I've been worried sick all night, praying decade after decade for you."

"You called Shelly's mom?" That sarcastic question haunted me for years. As if it had been her fault and not mine. As if I wasn't to blame for lying to her and making her a frantic wreck.

Oh, the way I spoke to my beautiful mom! I replayed my vocal tone over and over again. All she wanted was my honesty and time.

After my "incident" and after Mom's diagnosis, we started praying together every Sunday night. I couldn't control her cancer, but we could pray for a cure.

After she died, I refused to pray alone.

The guilt was too much to bear. I wanted to be punished, to carry the sinful burden of having hurt my mother. She loved me more than anything. Dad loved me, too, but he was lost after her death. We roamed the rooms of our home in silence, not even knocking on the bathroom door to see how long one of us was going to be; we just waited until we heard the door open to take our turn. After all those teen years of wanting to stay away from my parents, I just wanted my dad to hold me, to sit next to me, and to eat cookies and cry together. But he didn't know how to do that. Neither did I. The magnolia petals sat like sludge for a long time. We let them.

It was at age twenty-one in my junior year of college when I took a psychology class and thought I understood the distance between my dad and me. I explained to him the five stages of grief, and instead of applying the new knowledge to myself, I offered him advice and guidance. As if I knew anything about losing a spouse, a soulmate. Unfortunately, that, too, would come.

"And a thirty-something is curious and wants family answers?" he finished.

"A thirty-something is looking for meaning in her times of uncertainty."

There was brief silence before he spoke.

"I'm a widower, Mimma. I understand the 'uncertainty' that that brings, and I understand the daily sorrow. I wish I could take away your pain and tell you that everything is going to get better. It will, but you'll never be the same." He looked directly into my eyes. "You need to move on, though. Not from Vinny, but from sadness."

I couldn't chew. I couldn't speak. Dad looked away and cleared his throat.

"My nonno and his three brothers Pietro and Angelo and Vittorio built the bakery in the 1920s. I think it was '22. Of course, I'm named after my nonno, Paolo, who married my grandma, Anna Weber, a German resident of Hull House."

"The Jane Addams place, right?"

"Yes." Dad played with the basil on his plate, and his eyes glassed over as if in a dream. "Zio Vittorio, one of the brothers, was the GOAT." I rolled my eyes as if still in my rebellious stage, and Dad grinned with delight because he accurately used the modern reference to the Greatest of All Time. "We were blessed to have him with us for so long. What a character. And so many stories. He never married and oversaw the family business until he died at one-hundred years old. Do you remember him?"

"Vaguely."

"Then there was Angelo who was Cousin Maria's nonno. And the eldest of the brothers was Pietro, who, from what I always heard, was the hothead of the *famiglia*."

"So Russo Bakery was started by the four boys: Pietro, Angelo, Vittorio, and Paolo."

"Yes. After Pietro moved his family away, everyone pitched in for generations, until one by one the siblings and offspring started moving away, too."

"When it was your dad's turn to take over the shop, why did he relocate instead of staying close to the business?" I asked.

"Family folklore says that my mother wanted to get away from the Russos, which is believable because my father's family was a handful, but Mamma never spoke of it. Zio Vittorio said Mamma was jealous of a woman named Florence Scala whom my dad supported in her bid for alderperson. He was on her campaign committee, spent too much time away from home, and Zio claimed that my dad was becoming more rebellious than my mom could take. Cousin Maria, on the other hand, said that Mamma wanted to move because she couldn't stay in a city where her childhood home on Marshfield was demolished for a parking lot. Upheaval for Little Italy was a daily concern for Mamma's family as well as the whole neighborhood. It wasn't until I graduated from University of Illinois-Chicago that I heard that story, which explained Mamma's tears every morning when I took the train to the city."

"Dad, that makes perfect sense!" I had never thought about that. Between the construction of the expressway and the building of the UIC campus, I knew development devastated the community, but I had never thought about my grandma being personally affected.

"What a shame," I said. "I didn't know, Dad."

"No one knew. My mom didn't share her life or feelings with us. She did, though, make it clear that she wanted her children to assimilate more than she did, and she demanded that everyone call us by our American names. My relatives refused. To everyone but a Russo, I'm Paulie instead of Paolo, and my sister was Josie instead of Giuseppina." He took a forkful of tomato and then he added, "'*Ostinata*' is what Vittorio used to say."

"Did Grandma approve of your marriage to Mom? I mean, they were so different."

"Ha! No, she did not approve, but they tolerated each other. You have to understand, Toni, that *my* mom was a kind of outsider with the Russos, but *your* mom was a family favorite."

"So, when did *you* actually take things over?"

"Just after you were born. Your mom loved the bakery and she loved *mia familia*. She grew up with all of us. So, my wife Amelia and my sister Josie and my cousin Maria were best friends. "Le Terzine" they called themselves because their birthdays were near each other, and they thought of themselves as not biological but poetic triplets. They loved running that shop, and I loved that they loved it—I could keep my accounting job. I basically did the books when I was away from the store, and I did what I was told when I was there. Maria lived upstairs and took care of Zio who was still opinionated about how things were done. They all got along and were happy, so that made me happy."

My only dream is the same one I've had since we started dating. To make you happy.

"Family was everywhere. Upstairs, next door, around the corner. If my dad had his way, I think we would have stayed on Taylor Street where he found a lot of joy."

Could I bring back that joy for them? For me?

Tuesday

A thin dust cloud hung in the air, and I sneezed when the chalky powder touched my nose. The crowbar-carrying construction crew, some clad in particle masks and goggles and gloves, were already hard at work when I arrived at 7am, and excitement rushed through my veins. I had expressed my wish for exposed brick, but Richie explained that nothing was guaranteed until the demo began. And there it was!

The west side of the space already showed the interior brick, and I ran my hand along a row of blocks, thinking of the men who had laid them one by one. My fingers jumped over each stud.

"Be careful with the wooden frame," I instructed the workers. "I'm told it's original to the building."

"You actually want to keep these old studs, Toni?"

"Of course! I can breathe new life into them. Repurpose them into shelves or a tabletop."

It's what I was attempting to do with my own self, breathe new life into a shattered one.

"I thought you said you wouldn't get in the way." Richie was entering the room with a sledge hammer and motioned for me to come to him. "I'm getting ready to take down the partition here. Want to take a swing?" he asked.

"I hear this is good therapy," I answered while extending my hand to grab the tool. It was heavier than expected, and since there was no other instruction than to take a whack at the wall, I thought about all the other walls I was ready to knock down, the personal ones. *Bitterness, doubt, disappointment. Why is it so easy to rattle off the emotions that are getting in the way of my happiness?* I grasped it with both hands—*emptiness*—brought it to my right side—*fear*—and thrust the heavy metal end as mightily as I could against the wall. The reward was a light dent, and we laughed. "I think I need to get to the gym before making a career at demolition," I said before holding out the hammer to Richie.

"Give it one more try, slugger," he encouraged, pointing at the wall. "Don't hold anything back."

I took a deep breath and put all my strength into the swing. *Moving on doesn't mean letting go.* Whack! This time the hit made a hole. A small hole, but still more than a dent.

"Thatta girl!" This time Richie accepted the hammer when I offered it, and we both smiled. "We'll take it from here, Toni."

He called a couple of the crew to help him bring down the partition, and with the new strength, it took all but thirty minutes to see what I could only imagine a half hour before. The space was vast. Even with the floors marked for the office and bathroom and storage, I was pleased with the area and envisioned the bookcases and sitting section and rows upon rows of children's stories, literary novels, historical fiction and nonfiction, biographies, poetry. More studs stood like a skeleton of the past, revealing what Richie had been speculating: along the east wall of the old kitchen was a three-foot closet. He nodded to the worker who was ready to smash the plaster. BAM! Withdraw. A throw over the shoulder. BAM! Withdraw. A throw over the shoulder. BAM!

What is that?

Pieces of gypsum board were torn from the studs, and then the crew pulled away another section. Behind the wall was the depth of three feet of empty space like a vacant pantry without any shelves. More sections were removed until only the partition's wooden frame stood. *What's hanging on the wall?* Richie and I looked at each other simultaneously. "Not quite the best location for an art gallery," Richie joked as we walked through the stud frame to get a close look at the surprising sight.

The faded painting hung askew on the exposed brick, a veil of decades-old grime clinging to the cracked glass encased within a tattered, wooden frame. With soft cloths we wiped and dusted. What was revealed was an image of a quaint village scene, a cobblestone street that connected cement walkways, flagstone staircases, and brick-lined entryways. Contrasting earth tones were marked by gray mortar outlines, but the cascading grapevines along the buildings' archways and facades showed aged vibrancy in the violet fruits and emerald leaves.

"Isn't that something," Richie remarked, staring.

"How cool is this!" I grabbed my phone from my pocket and dialed my father. "Dad, you have to come down to the shop and see something."

Holding his chin with his forefinger across his lips, Richie stood. "Why the heck would they wall up that painting?"

I have no idea. I didn't want to apply too much cleaning pressure on the piece, sure of its fragility, but I was hopeful that the outer cracks and breaks caused minimal harm to what lay beneath and within.

"Most of the damage is to the frame and glass, but the artwork seems intact," my thoughts spoke out loud.

Dad came through the front door before the contractor responded. He looked around at the vacant room. "This explains the racket down here," he said, putting a hand over his nose and mouth. "Impressive."

"Not as impressive as this, Dad. Keep walking, but be careful."

My father took a moment to feel the exposed brick. I could see the grin. It really was beautiful. Then he stepped over the piles of debris, shook hands with Richie, and gave me a hug. I pointed to the wall behind him. "Look there."

He turned and stared at the painting. "What *is* that?"

"Good question. I said the same thing."

As if pulled in its direction, Dad wasn't paying attention to the debris on the floor. His eyes were transfixed. His hands reached out to the purple spheres as they descended across the painting's edge, letting his fingers trace lines in the dust. "*Gaglioppo,*" he whispered.

From the top to the bottom of the painting, he let his fingers glide through the faded green foliage and purple globes until his middle tip touched a black smudge in the corner of the vines. I watched him use his thumb to rub away the grime gently.

Paolo Russo

"That's my grandfather."

*　*　*

When Richie and his guys were done for the day, we cleaned the painting's frame the best we could. I took pictures of the art before draping it in plastic, not yet removing the canvas from its protective glass casing.

My dad pondered for hours the recognizable scene. "It's a familiar place, Toni, but I can't put my finger on it."

We went upstairs to the living room and broke out the photo albums. We paged through generations of black and white portraits from the twenties, thirties, forties. I repeatedly looked at my dad and then at the photographs. The resemblances were uncanny.

After Mom passed, I rarely looked directly at my dad. I couldn't bear to witness the painful expressions, but one day as we sat at the kitchen table, I caught myself studying his face with its widow's peak hairline and espresso eyes, long lashes, and slight bags under the lower lids that cast delicate shadows on his olive complexion. When I told him he had a mysterious look about him, he stared back at me, smiled, and said it was genetic. He was right. Almost every face in those pictures had those same features. Male and female, young and old, my ancestors' wardrobes changed through the decades but not those eyes. From the cloche to pillbox hats, from newsboy caps to fedoras, no one could escape the Russo trademark of mysterious eyes and widow's peaks.

"Those are some strong genes," I commented.

"There's no denying that you're mine," he said as he touched my forehead's V point. "But I'm focusing on the backgrounds more than the people."

"What did you mean when you said *gaglioppo*?"

"The *gaglioppo* grape comes from Calabria, and it makes a soft, red wine. Years ago, when relatives came to visit, they brought several bottles, and Zio Vittorio told story after story about working in the *gaglioppo* vineyards when he was a young man."

"Is that him?" I wondered, pointing at a photo with a baker standing behind the pastry counter. The man was wearing a white v-neck t-shirt and an apron tied around his waist. He was waving at the person behind the camera with a dusting of flour on his hands and arms, and he was beaming with a smile that appeared to be mid-laughter. His short, dark hair accentuated his widow's peak.

"Yep," my father confirmed. "That's Zio."

"He's handsome," I said.

"He's a Russo," Dad replied with a nudge to my side. "What did you expect?"

Halfway through the fifth album, Dad pointed at a page and tapped the center picture. "That's it."

"Who are they?" I asked.

"That's my dad in the flannel shirt, and that's his cousin Marco in the soldier's uniform next to him."

"And Marco is Maria's father?"

"That is correct."

Dad took a piece of paper and scribbled names on it to form a descendant chart. He pointed to the first column. "Just to make our relations clear, here's my grandpa's name Paolo who had my dad Antonio who had me." He then pointed to the second column. "Here's his brother's name Angelo who had Marco who had Maria."

"Got it," I responded.

Dad went back to the album and lifted the plastic film. He scraped his nail on the corner of the photo to release it from the page. Written on the back side was "*Welcome Home, Marco - Jan, 1946.*"

"He must have just returned from fighting in WWII."

"Do you recognize the room they're standing in?"

The figures were standing in front of a Christmas tree, lights appearing like white circular discs on gray, sparse branches that separated enough to reflect the camera flash on the window behind it. The bay window. *The bay window with the mismatched trim.*

"The trim!" I noticed. "They're standing *here* where we're sitting!"

"And look at the wall on the left."

Only half the painting was visible in the shot, but there was no doubt about it. The discovered artwork downstairs was once on full display on the wall of the very room we were in.

We returned to the album, and for the next couple pages, the painting was in view for every photo taken in the living room through 1946. And then the wall was empty.

"Someone must have moved the painting to the bakery," Dad realized. "Maybe they wanted more people to see it."

"And then someone decided to wall it up, so that no one could ever see it again," I inserted.

*   *   *

Back at my apartment, I uploaded onto my computer the pictures I had taken of the painting. I zoomed in to every detail. The flagstone walkway had more texture when seen close up. The archway appeared more rustic with defined cracks, and the grapevines moved about with no beginning or end. Scrolling slowly towards the corner's signature, I magnified the words on my screen. It became blurrier with each click, but there was something strange about the lettering. The "l" in "Paolo" looked misshapen with a point at the bottom. *Is that supposed to look like an arrow?* It appeared to be more than a lowercase "L." Or maybe I just needed some sleep. It had been a long day.

Before going to bed, I did something I hadn't done since I was a teenager. I took out my "mom box" with little mementos of cards and jewelry, her old apron and slippers. I thought what I was looking for could be found there. After a quick reminder to pray to St. Anthony, I realized that I was searching in the wrong place. I opened my top dresser drawer and pulled out a small blue velvet pouch that had been collecting dust. I knelt down next to my reading chair and opened the soft covering, gingerly taking the beads into my hand. *I don't think I remember how this goes, Mom, so give me a little grace tonight.* I could only recite the *Hail Mary* prayer, but I mumbled it fifty-three times. When I finished my version of the rosary, I didn't feel spiritually enlightened at all; however, knowing that my mom's fingers had touched every bead that I touched—well, I hadn't felt that kind of connection in a long time.

WEDNESDAY

I turned the page on my desk calendar: July 23. By this time in any other year, I'd be thinking about curriculum goals and supply lists, but I had submitted my teacher resignation in June, after the last eighth grade class had graduated and everyone was settled into vacations and summer projects. No fanfare or going away party, no goodbyes to faculty with whom I'd bonded over student-driven policies and cross-curricular brainstorming. Stella was the only colleague I had told in advance, but that was because we knew each other from college, before having worked together. No one else knew, and many wouldn't know until August when they reconvened for the next school year. It was easier that way, and I had grown used to breaks without closure since the day Vinny died. Anyway, with the goings on that transpired in the past two days at the shop, my mind and heart opened their doors to a new path that I had never anticipated.

After running errands, I made a stop at the storage unit where my inventory was kept on six-foot bookshelves obtained from the local high school library that had renovated and downsized their collection a couple years ago. The bookstore had been a dream for so long, but not anymore. Now a fast-forward button was being held down, and I had to keep up. I had confessed on many occasions that I was not the most methodical person in the world, using my own "logical" system when a more efficient system would have been a better choice. I studied for classes I enjoyed first, when I should have gotten the tough subjects out of the way beforehand. I cleaned what I saw in front of me without thinking of my dad's process of top to bottom. Knowing this about myself, the books took a long time to record; there had to be a quicker approach, but the result was satisfying nonetheless. Stock from rummage sales and estate sales and library sales and bookstore liquidation sales—"We'll be closing our doors next week. Everything must go" the signs read—and I prayed that wouldn't be my near future. Family and friend donations, local author donations, historical society donations. Thousands of books had been collected and boxed by category and subcategory. Soon the day would come to find them all a new home, a new home that existed on the first level of my dad's present home, in our ancestors' old home.

It was after 6pm by the time I finished my inventory additions to the Point of Sale system and met the website designer for dinner down the street at Hawkeyes. Taylor Street was active with couples on their way to The Rosebud, a legendary fine dining establishment, and families hurrying to Mario's Italian Lemonade, a neighborhood staple that relieved the heat of the Chicago summer sun. Luckily, the parking gods saved a spot in front of our shop. "Rock star parking" Vinny used to say when we caught a break at any of our city destinations. I glanced up again at the terracotta top before walking into my soon-to-be bookstore.

Wow. The floors were covered in dust, but the walls were dramatically exposed. The entire crew had to have lent a hand in the cleaning and sealing of it all. The result was a ton of residue beneath my feet, yet a stunning space that felt like an old hug. Just as stunning was the new south partition wall with an archway that led to the back office and storage room. "Reminds me of the archway in the painting," I whispered, and an idea flashed as I imagined a flagstone walkway from the store entrance to the south wall. *Note to self: ask Richie what he thinks of that.*

The butcher block paper that shrouded the bay window would soon get replaced with a new logo, but presently, the covering cast a shadow within. The sun's position was above the building, and dimness would grow towards darkness as the next hours passed. I was grateful for that exact moment when light was still an ally so that the artwork wrapped in plastic was still clearly visible. *I love that Richie hung this back up for me to see when I arrived.*

As I approached it, I noticed a set of footprints in the floor dust, toes pointed towards the painting as if the person who owned those prints had been standing, just like me, staring in wonder at the beautiful discovery. They didn't look like boot prints, so I assumed it had been my father. I felt as if we were museum visitors, Dad and me, reflecting on a masterpiece at the Art Institute.

Remembering the signature I had scrutinized the night before, I took a closer look at the real thing. That "l" looked like an arrow pointing downward, so my eyes followed the direction to the floor and back up to the painting. After a few more minutes, I stepped back into the footprints to see what the other admirer saw, or didn't. That's when something strange caught my eye. There seemed to be a slightly wider groove in one of the floorboards under my feet. The dust settled a bit more thickly in that groove than elsewhere, like the difference between a fine-tip and broad-tip marker line. I knelt and brushed away the chalky powder, and then I ran my finger over the groove. It wasn't smooth. Grabbing a flashlight from the toolbox against the back door, I ran my finger over the groove again, and this time, I held the light in my other hand.

"Do I feel a nail?" I questioned out loud.

I blew away the dust that remained, and sure enough, some kind of nail or screw was buried lengthwise in the groove. *Huh.*

I found a cloth, dampened it with bottled water, and returned to my spot. Wiping down the groove, I noticed another lengthwise object about a foot away, and then another object another foot away.

"What the heck?"

I kept wiping and realized that there were three screws lined up. As I stared at the groove, something else came to my attention: a thin, perpendicular line that led straight across the other floorboards all the way to the wall. So thin was the cut into the oak that barely any dust settled in it. The human eye would never see it without knowing it was there. And there were two of them: one above the first screw and one below the last screw.

"Could this possibly be a door in the floor?"

My cellphone's doorbell ringtone sounded a loud ding-dong, and I nearly jumped out of my skin. I answered the incoming call without even checking the number.

"Hi, Toni. Are you ok?"

"Yes. Who is this?" I took a deep breath to regain my composure.

"This is James. You sound startled."

"I guess that's a good description. The ring scared the heck out of me."

"Sorry about that. I just wanted to touch base about dinner tomorrow, but I think I caught you at a bad time."

"No, James. This is a fine time. I'm the one who should apologize. I'm at the bookstore, and I found something odd, and I was all in my head when you called."

"Something odd?" he asked.

"Yeah. I've come to realize that old buildings uncover old things."

"Back in my cable days, I used to find strange things behind the walls. Especially old newspapers. I was fascinated every time the walls talked like that."

"You're right. When walls come down, we learn things. I have a feeling I'm on a journey I didn't know I was on. This is fascinating, all right."

"Anything I might be able to help you with?"

"If you ever discovered a door in a floor, then yes, but I doubt that you know anything about that."

"Was the building around in the 1920s?"

I paused. "Yes."

"Did you try opening the door?"

"I just found it, and I don't see a handle."

"It could be a door to an underground tunnel."

"Are you kidding me?"

"I'm completely serious. I installed a lot of cable in old homes. For houses built in the 1920s, sometimes there were crawl spaces under floor doors, and sometimes there were underground escape routes used in the Prohibition Era. No joke."

"Huh. That's actually believable. You might be onto something, James."

"It would be pretty cool if that's what it turns out to be."

I looked back to the painting on the wall.

"I have another question for you."

"Shoot."

"Do you know anything about 1920s art?"

"Art is not one of my specialties. I appreciate it, but I can't ever understand it."

"I can't, either."

"If we're still on for tomorrow night," James started, subtly getting back to his original agenda, "I'd like to hear about these demo adventures. It sounds like you've had some eventful days since we met on Monday."

"We are still on for tomorrow. Have you ever been to Hawkeyes?"

"Once or twice. Good choice. What time works for you?"

"How about 6:00?" I asked.

"Perfect. Should I pick you up or meet you there?" Then he added, "Whatever you're comfortable with."

Is this guy always so polite?

"I can meet you there. I'll most likely be walking over."

"We're all set, then, Toni. I'm looking forward to seeing you again."

"Ok. See you."

I hung up. *Ok? He's told you two times that he's looking forward to seeing you, and all you have to say is "ok." Toni, you can be so darn rude!*

Ready or not, I was apparently going on a date.

*　*　*

A Google search back home for "door in floorboards" led me to new phrases like *"access hatches"* and *"trapdoors,"* mostly for purposes of getting to electrical and plumbing sources, or as an access to a basement or crawlspace. I decided to wait until the next day to broach the subject with Richie and my father. Maybe that's all there was to it. Or maybe James was right.

My next Google search was "instructions on how to pray the rosary." I couldn't concentrate. I tried to recite the first prayers, but my mind drifted. *I'm sorry, Mom.* I then made a quick Sign of the Cross.

I didn't get much sleep that night. My thoughts and eventual dreams focused on the "what ifs" of yet another mysterious discovery.

THURSDAY

My father was a creature of habit, so I called early to catch him making coffee after returning from morning Mass at Holy Family Church.

"Don't usually get calls from you at this hour. Everything ok, Mimma?"

"Everything is fine, Dad, but I have a couple questions for you."

* * *

"I feel the hinge screw," Dad announced, squatting next to me and tracing the groove with his forefinger.

"There should be three."

Dad put his right knee to the floor and continued to run his finger the length of the groove.

"Yep," he said at the second screw, and another "yep" when he got to the third.

"And look at the cross lines at the top and the bottom," I pointed out.

Dad squinted before saying, "I don't see them."

"You have to look real close," I said.

I ran my finger along the line below the last screw.

"Ah. Now, I see it."

We stood, and after my father brushed the dust from his knee, he put an arm around my shoulder and kissed me on the forehead.

"You can't imagine the excitement this would have brought," he said. "Le Terzine would have been all over this."

He took a handkerchief from his pocket and dabbed his misty eyes.

"I started praying Mom's rosary beads," I told him.

"That's beautiful, Mimma. She's with us. Every day. Right now, even. I can feel her."

Richie's truck was backing into the parking space in front of the shop, and Dad put his handkerchief away. "I can't wait to see his reaction."

It was a tight squeeze that was testing Richie's parallel parking skills, so we walked out to the sidewalk to greet him.

"I never had a welcome committee before this project. Good morning, Russos!"

"Toni's got another revelation," Dad blurted out before I could share the news.

"Why doesn't that surprise me?"

I held open the front door, and with a coffee in one hand and a toolbox in the other, Richie entered. "*Grazie*," he said with a smile and a nod.

I led us to the floorboard and told my story of the previous evening.

"I don't see a hole to lift it. Do you, Richie?"

He didn't respond right away, but after a few minutes he said, "Here."

It was barely visible, a circular line that blended into the wood grain like a notch.

"It's been glued in," he explained, "but this is definitely an access hole."

"I can't believe it," Dad said, eyes opened wide, making the Sign of the Cross.

"Well, believe it, Paulie. Mind if I get a drill?"

I responded without hesitation. "You said you never knew what you'd find behind walls, and look what happened with the painting. Let's see what we find below the floors, Richie."

He opened his toolbox and chose the largest bit he could find. "Here we go, Russos."

It seemed blasphemous to cut into the beautiful oak planks, but we stepped back as Richie put on his goggles and placed the drill tip in the center of the notch. Small chips jumped into the air amid the whir of the tool. Once the hole was made, he poked his fingers through and gave a tug.

"Wishful thinking that it would be that easy." He stood up and evaluated the scene. "Ok. If we want to lift this, we'll need to cut along the seams to remove whatever adhesive is holding the floorboards in place." He positioned a flashlight directly above the hole. "I can't see anything. I have no idea what's down there."

"Let's go for it," I said, a twinge of excitement running through me the way it had in my youthful days when absorbed in all-afternoon readings of Trixie Belden and Nancy Drew stories.

"If you don't mind, I'm gonna call the crew to delay our start. I don't want to move forward with clean-up and painting until we spend some time on this floor."

"Good idea," Dad replied. "How about I get us more coffee?"

"Would love some, Paulie."

"Of course," I agreed.

Dad left and Richie went to the back to make a few phone calls. I took the opportunity to text James an update. *Wait. What does it mean that I want to share this moment with James?* Claire would be happy that I kept in contact with a "man of interest." *Is that what I should call him?*

I wrote, "*Getting ready to open the hatch.*"

James replied, "*Keep me posted! I thought about it all night!*"

At first, I read the "it" as "you," thinking James had thought about *me* all night. I felt my heart race for a moment, and for some reason, it bothered me that I couldn't envision James in deep thought while trying to get rest. Whether his thinking was focused on me or the store, I found myself wondering what his home looked like, what he, himself, looked like when he went to bed, when he slept, when he woke in the morning.

"Whoa," I told myself, abruptly halting those thoughts. *You've got yourself wondering about a lot of things, Toni! Stay focused on the floor.*

I stood over the trapdoor. Once realizing it was there, the outline became obvious to me, just like the rooftop terracotta that would probably be seen each time I pulled up in front of the building. I thought back to my third grade teacher sharing optical illusion books with us, and my classmates hovering over the images, debating whether the picture was a bunny or a duck, an old woman or a young woman. We argued until we saw the opposite view, and then it was difficult to return our brains to our original images. It was such a great lesson on perception that I copied the activity in my own classroom.

My eyes returned to the painting on the wall, still protected by plastic, and I was once again drawn to the signature, the "l" that pointed downward. I covered my mouth and muttered, "Oh, my God!" It pointed to the drilled hole in the ground!

"Now what?" Richie said, reentering the room and putting his phone in his shirt pocket.

"The 'L' in my great grandfather's name looks like an arrow pointing to the hole, doesn't it?"

Richie stepped up close. "Looks like a dagger to me."

"Ok, so it's a dagger pointing to the hole. Doesn't that seem strange?"

"Ha! We just demolished a wall and found a picture that was painted by your great grandfather and his signature shows a dagger symbol that could be the same symbol used in a Black Hand threat." He laughed out loud. "Yeah, Toni. I think the whole thing is strange."

"'A Black Hand threat?'"

"Sure. Prior to the Chicago Outfit, the Mano Nera, or the Black Hand as they were mostly called on the streets, was an extortion group from Sicily that threatened people, mostly other Italians, whom they could scare into giving them money. They sent letters to those poor immigrants. Blackmail. Those letters always included death symbols. A dagger was one of them."

Dad returned with fresh cups of coffee.

"Have you ever heard of the Black Hand?" I asked.

"Zio Vittorio mentioned the Black Hand every once in a while. It wasn't his favorite subject, but there was definitely a brother who was blackmailed. That's all I recall."

"Many families from this neighborhood have a Mano Nera story in their past," Richie explained as he accepted his coffee refill from my dad.

"Thank you, boss." He took one sip, put down the cup, and walked to the floorboard. "Let's see what we got down there."

We all slipped goggles onto our faces while Richie started up the electric saw. He began with the thin line along one end of the door. He gave another tug on the access hole, and there was a slight give.

"I'll do the same thing on the other side."

Richie repeated the sawing and then drilled a new access hole at that end. We both tried to tug on the access holes, and my heart pounded with each give.

"If you help me, Toni, we might be able to pry open the long groove," Richie said. "We just can't step directly on top of the door planks." He walked away and retrieved a couple crowbars. "Here's one for you. You can pry from the bottom, and I'll pry from the top at the same time."

"You remember what I did with the sledgehammer, right?"

"You didn't have the adrenaline you have now." Richie smiled. "I think you've got this."

And that was that. Little by little, we each pried several inches-turned-into-a-foot.

"I think we should tug again," I said. "Or am I being impatient?"

"Let's do it," Richie replied.

The creaking sound of the door breaking loose excited me—enthralled *us*. For how many years was this thing sealed? It lifted. The tired screws bent. Except for the cobwebs that draped the interior side of the door, the space was entirely black.

We grabbed a couple more flashlights. A step. Two. As the light illuminated this cavity under the floor, we were amazed to see a full wooden staircase that appeared to end with dirt ground.

I heard my father mutter "Sweet Jesus" before he counted out loud. "One, two, three, four, five, six, seven, eight. I've got eight stairs."

"That's what I count, too, Dad."

"My curiosity says to get on down there, but my logic says the stairs might have deteriorated."

"You're not going anywhere, Paulie. I'll scout it out first. In my line, I've fallen off ladders taller than this, and I've been just fine. I'll go down on my butt."

There were always surprises when tearing down walls. That's what Richie told Dad when they first met about this project. Of course there was excitement, but with anticipation came worry. *Daggers might have been associated with the Black Hand, but secret tunnels were usually associated with the mob. What if we find something terrible?*

Richie brushed away the webs and then maneuvered himself into a sitting position while Dad and I shined our flashlights to guide his way. He put his feet on the first stair and applied pressure. "So far so good." Then he brought his feet to the second stair and applied some pressure. "I'm going for it, Russos." He brought his butt onto the top stair and his feet to the stairs farther down, applied pressure, and continued the trek. When he got to the bottom, he flashed his light around and then called to us. "Let me walk it up to be sure it's stable for you to join me." He carefully took one step at a time, and when he returned to us, he said, "I think you've got yourself an underground tunnel."

I descended next, my heart was fluttering faster with each downward step, and I experienced a quick déjà-vu moment that caused me to catch my breath. I had never been claustrophobic prior to Mom's funeral, but I had never witnessed the lowering of a casket before that event, either. My mind believed that her soul was eternally safe and that her physical body was simply a holding space on Earth, but I found it difficult to watch the casket close, get bolted shut and positioned above the dugout grave, dropped inch by inch into the ground, no longer visible, gone. For weeks after the service, I had woken in the middle of the night, startled and needing to catch my breath, needing my father's consolation and security to regain my composure, and he never missed my call no matter how soft my teenage whimper sounded. "Dad," I mumbled quietly as I reached the bottom stair.

He was already making his own descent, and Dad squeezed my hand when he got to the final step, himself. We didn't need to see each other or speak. We both knew what I was feeling.

We were in complete darkness with the exception of our flashlights. It was a short tunnel on account of the brick wall that, according to Richie, was probably built with the 1946 renovations. Richie explained, "If it was a direct route with no curves, this heads south. Where to, I haven't the faintest clue."

There was nothing to see except the dirt floor and cement walls. No lights, no markings, nothing. And then…

"There's something under the staircase," Dad said, shining his flash onto a box that was blending into the darkness.

Richie reached for it, a black metal box about three feet long and two feet wide. There were black handles on either end. "You've got another discovery on your hands, and this job has turned into the most interesting one of my career."

*　*　*

After lugging the box upstairs, we closed the floor opening and set the chest on a card table next to the access door in the shop. A padlock needed to be broken, and we left it to Richie again to use a hammer to coax it open. "I think you should have the honor of opening this, Paulie."

My dad raised the creaking lid. On the inside cover, someone had scratched "La Famiglia Russo, 1915, da Cosenza a Chicago." Dad lifted out an instrument case, unfastened the latch, and revealed an old mandolin. The tag inside said *"Angelo Russo."* As my father inspected the strings and neck and bowl back, I picked up a book lying beneath the instrument. It was a sketchbook with the name on the hardcover of *"Paolo Russo,"* and the pages were filled with pencil drawings similar to the painting that watched over us, quaint village scenes with homes nestled one upon the next, some walkways, some gardens. Another book left in the box was a bible, a family bible, and the pages were so fine I was afraid to turn them. Each of the boys' names and birthdates was scrawled on the first page in faded ink, and little scraps of paper protruded throughout the scriptures, like sticky notes of modern times. I opened one of those tabs, and what I found was not a reading marker, but a recipe card for "*I biscotti della nonna.*" The name "*Pietro Russo*" was inscribed on the back. I carefully flipped the delicate bible pages and found more recipe cards written in Italian. The last item was a brown folder filled with hand-written pages. On the cover were the initials "V. R." etched in gold ink, and the entire file was tied with a piece of brown suede. Like the bible, the pages were thin and frail.

"These items may have been what they came to the U.S. with," Dad said.

"But why keep them hidden down here?" I asked.

* * *

At dinner that night, I told my day's story to James and left off with, "I wish I knew why the brothers abandoned these treasures in a box under the stairs of a hidden tunnel." I took a sip of my wine. "Sounds crazy, right?"

"Maybe for safe keeping," he said.

"Safe keeping from what? Or from whom?"

"Didn't your dad say that someone feared the Black Hand?"

"Zio Vittorio told him that. My dad took out an old victrola that was packed away in a bedroom closet, and he's been playing Vittorio's Italian records, listening to his ancestors' music while looking at every sketch that his grandfather drew. I don't think he's looking for answers to anything more than connections that might have been lost through the years." I lifted my glass to take another drink, but it was empty. James picked up the bottle and poured. "Thank you," I said. We clinked glasses, and then I continued, "Dad knows enough Italian to read the recipe cards, but Vittorio's writing and the bible are more difficult. If there's info to find, we'll have to wait until we find a translator."

James gagged but caught himself with an immediate napkin to the mouth. "A translator?" he choked out.

"Are you ok?"

"Your line about getting a translator made me nearly spit out my drink. *Insegno italiano.* You know that I teach Italian, yes?"

I gave a puzzled look. *What the hell is wrong with me? He's a foreign language teacher! Did I never ask him which languages he taught? Did he tell me and I didn't pay attention? The terracotta. For heaven's sake, Toni, are you that self-absorbed?*

"Toni, I don't just speak Italian; I can read and write the language, as well." He smiled and touched my hand, briefly. "I'd be honored to translate for you."

My face felt flush with embarrassment, but James put me at ease.

"Thank you. I just might take you up on that."

*　*　*

When I walked into my father's apartment, he was sitting at the kitchen table paging through the old family bible and the recipe cards inside.

"Hey, Dad."

"I thought you were on a date."

"I had dinner with a new friend, but I figured I'd stop by to see how you're doing, what you're thinking about with this whole situation."

"I'm doing fine. The situation is what it is, exciting and confusing. I assume we'll have to have Richie contact someone with the City to report the tunnel. Or maybe not. We'll see what he says."

"The mandolin is amazing, right? Did you know anyone in your family who played?"

My father looked through the corridor into the living room where the instrument lay in its open case on the couch.

"Everyone loved their music from the Old Country, but I don't remember any of my relatives being musically inclined. My dad used to talk about rolling up the rugs in the front room or in the homes of his cousins down the street, turning on the radio or victrola, and dancing their hearts out."

"This neighborhood was special," I said.

"I wish I could have grown up like that, a part of it all. Sometimes I get upset with my mom for taking us away. It was only a few towns over, but it wasn't the same. The kids I played with and went to school with had American names and spoke English in their homes. On Taylor Street, the kids spoke English at school and Italian at home. They went to Masses said in Italian. They listened to Italian music and followed family recipes and listened to their ancestors' stories. I became Paulie and never learned a word of Italian until I took it as a class in high school."

"How did you do?"

"I got a C and still can't speak more than the average American. Except for the swear words. I learned those at home and never forgot them."

I had to laugh at that one, and then I mentioned James. "My friend is an Italian teacher and offered to translate anything we need."

"James." Dad sat back in his chair and folded his hands in his lap. "Your new friend James."

"Dad, don't start." He leaned over and tousled my hair the way he did when I was a girl, after a volleyball win or choir concert, not caring if I was with friends, only being happy for his daughter. The hair messing annoyed me back then, but not anymore.

"You're not gonna tell me how the date went?"

"I think James is a new friend who happened to take me for dinner at the same time we need an Italian translator." *Do you believe in coincidence?*

"I'll let you off the hook tonight. Tomorrow, while the crew finishes what they have to do downstairs, I'll be right here making mostaccioli for this weekend's church festivities. Don't forget it's the Feast of St. Anne. Maybe you could invite your new friend over, and he could do some translating while he helps us bake."

"'Us?' I don't think I offered any baking help."

"Seeing you help your papà will make a good impression, Mimma."

"*Caulu!*"

Wagging his pointer finger at me, he reprimanded, "Don't forget that I understand that language." Who would have thought that the Calabresi call each other "cabbage"—*caulu*—as a putdown?

"I'm kidding. I'll have him meet us here tomorrow afternoon."

I gave *padre mio* a hug and a kiss on the cheek. "*Buonanotte*, Papà."

* * *

The wooden beads shone under the light of my reading lamp, shades of brown and burgundy, hints of gold. "In the name of the Father, and of the Son, and of the Holy Spirit."

FRIDAY

"In my opinion, that idea you had about a path from the entry to the archway partition is too much," Richie told me, referring to the flagstone walkway. "However, we could do a textured tile over the floor door, no? Maybe build some benches out of the studs like you wanted, and then commission a local artist to paint a mural replica of your great grandfather's picture so that this whole corner brings the art to life, three-dimensional-like?" He was brainstorming, but I visualized it.

"And your arch becomes the arch of the painting!" I exclaimed. "The reading nook would be *in* the picture? Richie, that's brilliant!"

He brushed his shoulder and tried to pat himself on the back.

"The grapevines—" I started.

"—the grapevines should be painted around the archway, and all through the room, right, Toni? Maybe some painted cracks in the wall that mimic the street scene, too."

I couldn't help noticing and voicing, "You're as excited about this as I am."

"Who wouldn't be? The thrill is contagious. This is a great story you got here, Toni, and I'm just happy to be part of it."

The screen door opened and then closed with a *click* as Dad entered with both hands full. He smiled and came near. "I'm feeling some good energy here. What are you talking about?" He handed us each a cup of fresh coffee.

Richie summed up the idea, and Dad stared at the bare space, envisioning it.

"I love it," he replied, still staring. "There's an amazing muralist in Chicago by the name of Cerone. Her agency can guide us."

"*Grazie*, Riccardo." Dad held up his coffee mug to gesture "cheers."

I leaned over and spoke in an intentionally loud whisper to Richie. "He can speak fluent conversational phrases."

"Ha! Well, then, *prego!*"

Dad patted his stomach. "I say thank you, and you say I look pregnant?"

"*Prego* means 'you're welcome,'" he laughed.

My father gave me a wink as Richie excused himself to the back office. "I have an instrument expert coming to see Zio Angelo's mandolin."

"Today?"

"Yes. He should be here any time now. I don't know about string pieces, but it looks like it's in good condition, don't you think?"

"It does to me, too. Are you thinking about selling it?"

"Heavens no. It needs to get appraised, and then we need to find the perfect place to display it. I don't want these treasures buried any longer."

"Agreed, Dad." We stood in silence, and then an image popped into my head. "What if the muralist added a life-size street musician on the wall before the arch—"

"—and hang the mandolin in the musician's arms, three-dimensional-like!"

"Everyone seems to know what I'm thinking! Yes!"

He put his hand on my shoulder and gave me a squeeze. "Toni, this store is going to be such a tribute to the Russo brothers."

"I think so, too, Dad," I looked at the floor and wall, all around me, and I smiled. "We'll need to find a way to recognize Vittorio and Pietro, too."

"It will come, Mimma. It will come."

"I've got the name of Helen Bruno, an associate of Cerone and a highly recommended muralist," Richie announced, reentering through the arch. "She sounds perfect for this project."

"Well, that was quick! Do we have contact info?" I asked.

"I'm already on it. I left a message on her answering machine." *It's all falling into place, Vinny. I think I'm on my way to happiness.*

"You've been a real blessing this week, Richie."

"It's been an interesting week to say the least, Paulie. By tomorrow, I'm hoping my crew will have the walls and floors ready for the next phase. We have the painters coming in the morning to give the base coat, and then we'll wait to hear from the muralist about what she'll need, if she accepts the project, if you like what she comes up with. The opening will be delayed, of course, but it will be worth it in the end."

"Can you believe this, Toni?"

I have an odd knack for recalling literature, not just characters and plots, but specific lines. When Dad asked if I could believe what was happening with the shop, I recited in my head a line from "Walden" by Henry David Thoreau: "if one advances confidently in the direction of his dreams, and endeavors to live the life which he has imagined, he will meet with a success unexpected in common hours." The passage felt right for the time, but my *"hours"* didn't feel *"common"* at all.

"I can believe it, Dad. I have a feeling this was all meant to be."

"Me, too." He patted me on the back. "Me, too."

"Do you still plan on baking today?"

"Of course. Is your new friend still planning on baking today?"

"James will be here by 2:00. *He* will translate. *I* will bake."

"I ordered enough strudel to feed an army, so he better bring an appetite."

"Oooh! From Pompei down the street?"

My father nodded.

"Chicken Parmigiana strudels?"

He smiled and nodded again.

"You are the best papà ever!"

"Thank you. It's easy to be the best papà when I have a daughter who is easy to please."

"*Prego.*"

We laughed.

*　*　*

Mr. Joe, as Dad called him, handed me his card when he entered the apartment ("Giuseppe 'Mr. Joe' Santino, Appraiser - Jewelry, Coins, Instruments"). There was no phone or address, just his name and title. When I asked why he didn't have all his information on there, he simply said, "People already know." I was always bad with age, but I guessed Mr. Joe was in his eighties, his white hair unkempt and curled about the face and neck. Despite no sign of balding, which surprised me for a man of that possible age, the deep wrinkles in his sun-drenched complexion and the translucence of his thin skin on the arms and hands gave light to his years. He carried a cane, but I considered that a precaution more than a necessity because he had managed the staircase up to Dad's apartment better than I, and his stature was more erect than my father's.

"This is what we call the mother of pearl inlay." The appraiser educated us about the mandolin as his fingers touched the design around the sound hole. "It's an intricate technique of cutting the outline in both the shells' inner layers as well as the wood, forming a puzzle piece to be placed together as precisely as possible. You want minimal glue, but anything extra gets buffed until smooth."

He lifted the mandolin to his nose. "This is rosewood, and it would need a lot of work if you wanted to play it, but for the sake of decoration, a little touch up would do." His hands glided over the bowl back, up the neck and to the front strings. "Very well made."

Setting the mandolin on the table, Mr. Joe reached into his jeans pocket and withdrew a magnifying glass. "The inside label is worn, but some details are clear. Made in Sicily, 1915, a Giuseppe Puglisi Reale & Figli Model." He chuckled to himself when adding the aside, "Good name." He continued his inspection. "Bone nuts and knobs." He gently returned the mandolin to its case. "How much do you want for it, Paolo?"

"I'm not looking to sell it," Dad quickly responded. "I'm interested in what it's worth before I hang it on the wall."

"To me? It's priceless," Mr. Joe said. "To an American buyer, about $500."

"That's good to know, Mr. Joe. I appreciate your service."

The old man was packing to leave when he leaned toward my father. "No display," he said.

"What do you mean?"

"Don't display it. Play it."

"I wouldn't know how. In my younger years, I toyed with a guitar but never got good at it," Dad explained.

Mr. Joe paused and then stated, "You *dis*covered the mandolin, you *un*covered its story, and now it's time to *re*cover. Recovery means bringing beauty back to life, the beauty of its music, the beauty of its soul."

*　*　*

"Ciao, Giacomo." My dad welcomed James into his home with a handshake, but my friend opened his arms for a hug. He won my father over immediately.

"Ciao, Signor Russo," James replied. *"Grazie per avermi invitato a casa Sua."*

The quizzical look on my father's face made me laugh, so I told him just to say *"prego."*

"My apologies," James said, placing his right hand on his chest. "I was thanking you for inviting me into your home."

"We are the ones who should be thanking you, James. And I guess my lack of conversation skills has been discovered," Dad chuckled.

"A lot of discovery happening around here," I added, and inside I thought about Mr. Joe's words of discovery, uncovery, and recovery. *I should give more reflection to the theme of self-discovery in literature. Paulo Coelho's Santiago was on such a journey in* The Alchemist. *What did he call it? A "Personal Legend?"*

"So I hear," said James.

"What?" I asked as I snapped out of my thoughts.

"I hear there's been a lot of discoveries around here." I nodded. Then James turned to Dad and said, "I'm looking forward to reading your great-uncle's pages, sir."

Dad motioned for us to come to the kitchen and sit. On the counter was an index box I bought for Zio Pietro's recipe cards. One of those cards was resting on top of the box, and the ingredient display was lined across the work surface.

"What do we have here?" James asked.

"Everything we need to bake mostaccioli."

"Aren't those for Christmas?"

"Ah, you have Southern roots! Most people in America think of mostaccioli as pasta and pasta only." Dad patted James on the back. "And yes, these are usually Christmas cookies, but we celebrate the Feast of St. Anne on Sunday at Holy Family Church, and since St. Anne is the grandmother of our Lord, we also celebrate grandparents, and since we are called the Church of the Holy Family, and since we found the original recipe card for these treasures, I made an exception to bring mostaccioli cookies to the festival."

"I apologize for questioning the cookie," James said sheepishly.

"No apologies! Delighted to know that you know what they are!"

James leaned over and whispered in my ear, "I'm not sure if I've made a good or bad first impression."

I smiled at him. "It's a good one. You had him with the hug."

"Well," Dad took the lead, "I'm thinking it might be best if we all lend a hand in the dough making, and while Toni and I cut and bake the cookies, you could read to us from Zio Vittorio's pages. What do you think?"

"Sounds good to me," James replied.

Dad handed us each an apron and then took the recipe card into his hands. He read the little note that was jotted in the top corner first. "Mostaccioli, a recipe from our Neapolitan neighbors." He took a moment to gaze at the writing of his ancestor, and then he brought the card to his lips, kissed it, and switched from sentimentality to business.

"First, James, I'd like you to line those four baking sheets with parchment paper from under the island."

"Yes, sir."

"And Toni, I need you to use this large mixing bowl to sift together the dry ingredients in the front row here: flour, baking powder, cloves, cinnamon, and cocoa."

"I'm on it, Papà."

Dad used a food processor to grind up the almonds, and when I was done sifting, he poured the nuts into my bowl. "Stir them in." I did as I was told.

"Looking good, crew." He motioned for James to join us at the counter. "I need you to beat the eggs now, James, and Toni, add the honey while he's doing that." There were bowls for everything, and once one bowl was used, it was placed in the oversized sink.

"How's this consistency?" James asked my dad, showing him the egg and honey mixture.

"*Bellissimo*! Bring that bowl over here so I can add the sugar," Dad told him.

James continued to beat the ingredients while I zested and juiced an orange and lemon. Dad looked on with a smile.

"Don't look all proud until we're done," I reminded him.

The bowls were combined and placed under the stand mixer, and the paddle churned it all into a soft and sticky dough.

Dad requested that I rinse the bowls and put them in the dishwasher. "If you remember one thing from your old man, Mimma, it's to clean as you go. Don't wait until the end."

"I couldn't agree with you more," chimed James, as he took the mixing paddle and bowl from in front of me. "I've got this, Toni."

Mom also concurred with Dad on this philosophy, not because it was her habit or nature, but because Julia Child said so. Mom and Aunt Josie used to have a television in the back of the bakery, but the only shows allowed on the screen were cooking programs, especially Julia Child and Lidia Bastianich. When these master chefs gave advice, my mom and aunt jotted down the helpful tidbits on index cards and hung them around the kitchen as reminders.

As James filled the dishwasher, Dad wiped and dried the counters and then reached for the flour container from the pantry. "Now the real fun starts." He sprinkled the flour on the counter surface and dropped a large spoonful of dough in the middle. He was a master at flattening it out before using a rolling pin.

"You seem to know what you're doing in the kitchen, Mr. Russo."

"I do enjoy being in the kitchen, James. And you can call me Paulie."

"Do you miss the bakery, Dad?" I asked.

"Let me put it this way, Toni. I find peace in cooking in my personal kitchen, but I have no desire to cook for a living. My profession is in accounting because that is what I'm good at. I found happiness in working a job and enjoying a passion at home. Some people think I'm crazy, but I don't find any joy in baking at the bakery."

"You're sure?" I asked.

"I'm positive. Your mom and aunt and Cousin Maria loved working and baking together every day. That was joy for them. Not for me."

When I was a young girl, one of my favorite pastimes was playing with Barbie dolls. I had three, and they all had dark hair and wore matching aprons. One day I put their hair up in ponytails and decided to use a brown marker to draw a little V on two of their foreheads, representing my dad's sister Aunt Josie's and his cousin Maria's widow's peaks. Then I took a red marker and drew a little heart on the chest of the third doll because my mom always told me I was in her heart. While all the other girls played with Barbie townhouses and campers and airplanes, I made my own kitchen out of cardboard boxes and pretended "Le Terzine" were baking up a storm. I wished I could have had best friends as Aunt Josie and Cousin Maria were to my mom.

"When did they stop working at the bakery?" James asked.

There was silence.

"Grab the rhombus cutter, Toni. This section of dough is ready for cutting."

More silence.

"I'm sorry if that was an uncomfortable question," James added.

"It's a legitimate question, James." Dad cut the rectangle of dough one by one into the rhombus shapes. "My sister, Toni's aunt, accepted a job at an elite Italian bakery in New York, and she got Cousin Maria an interview for a baker's apprenticeship. As much as my wife was distraught at both of them leaving, she was also excited for their new adventures and excited to have a place to visit. The unfortunate part of that plan was that the interview was scheduled for first thing in the morning on September 11, 2001."

"9/11," James whispered, and then he looked at me. "Your aunt and cousin were there?"

It had been a while since I'd thought back to that tragedy, how that event started the worst year of our lives. "Unfortunately," I responded, "they both died that day."

Dad added, "Amelia's ovarian cancer was newly detected at the time, and all three were gone within ten months."

James turned to me. "You told me about your mom, but I had no idea so much loss existed in so little time."

"It wasn't our best of times," I said, "but we survived and moved forward."

What did Claire say? You'll forever embrace your past, but allowing yourself to embrace your present is okay, too.

"I'm sure they're all together baking up a storm in Heaven, and probably looking down on us with pride for the mostaccioli!"

"Are we ready to bake, sir?"

"It's Paulie. And yes, we are ready."

*   *   *

The sheet pans were lined on the counter, and the smell of fresh baked cookies, especially the cinnamon and cloves, wafted from the oven. Everything was cleared away, the dishwasher was on, and the cooling racks were stacked on the kitchen island, ready for setting.

"I'll set a timer," Dad said, "and I think we ought to move to the dining room table for the reading."

"I'm ready," James said.

"Me, too," I added.

Dad set the brown folder in front of James. "It's fragile."

James placed a hand on the leather cover and ran his fingers over the V.R. initials. "I truly am honored to have this opportunity to translate your great-uncle's words." And with that he opened to the first page:

"*Promesse*," said James, touching the single word. "Promises."

1915 To write: My Maddalena made me promise to keep writing my poetic lines and stories. She so enjoyed my words. Oh, what a blessing and a curse that she left me in Cosenza! It is a blessing because without her I had nothing to keep me in Italy. So, I went with my brothers to America, just the way Mamma wished. It is a curse because I realized the seasickness I endured on the SS Berlin is similar to the lovesick ache I feel every day when I think of my departed love. Yes, she made me promise to keep writing, the way she found me when we met in the vineyards, the way I recited to her the private thoughts only my pen and paper had ever heard before. I will try to keep writing for my dearest, but my tears hit the page and smudge the words so often that my lines get confused.

James read slowly, his index finger gliding across the handwritten lines, and I was amazed at his ability to give an authentic voice to the script. His facial expressions—gentle eyes when speaking of the vineyards, and slight tilt of his head when saying "dearest"—brought Zio Vittorio to life.

All four of us brothers found our sponsor, a family acquaintance in New York, and we passed the tests for mental and physical ability, being processed the same day we arrived at Ellis Island. However, it took us weeks to find our way to the city of Chicago to meet Mamma's cousins and start a life of our own. We were cheated and robbed on numerous occasions, but we didn't show our growing fear, except when Pietro came to blows with a youth who tried to pick his pocket. We had to pull him off the poor child who was probably desperate. At first, the United States of America was not anything we dreamed of. Then we finally arrived in Chicago, and although the cousins did not expect us, they were helpful in finding us a place to stay temporarily at the corner of Taylor and May Streets. We learned that this neighborhood was called "Little Italy." We were, and continue to be, grateful to be surrounded by our language and culture. Maddalena and Mamma would have liked it here. I will keep my promise.

James paused. "It's smudged. I'm pretty sure I read that correctly."

"This is heartbreaking," I said, turning to my father. "Did Vittorio ever mention Maddalena?"

"Not to me. He was always the bachelor uncle, the one who took care of the family and the business and the home."

"It's well-composed," James said.

"I believe he was the only one with a formal education, so writing is not a surprise," Dad replied. James nodded, and Dad added, "Your translation is smooth and natural. You're talented, James."

His reply was a humble "*Grazie.*"

"Maybe I should be jotting down some notes as we go through this," I suggested.

"Grab a notebook out of the cabinet to your left. That's a good idea, Mimma."

I took out a notepad and a pen.

The timer went off, and Dad put in another tray of cookies while I finished my notes from the first entry.

"Ok, James. Ready to continue?" I asked.

"Absolutely. Here's another entry from 1915."

1915 To pray: I wanted this to be a good day. I wanted to watch the sun rise while sitting on the shore of Lake Michigan the way I did from the banks of the Busento River back home, and I wanted to recite some words of Christina Rosetti. This I did before heading to the railroads, but the day did not start as beautifully for others as it did for me. We have many bridges here in Chicago, and there was a tragedy by the Clark Street bridge this morning. News spread through the streets that a day trip for a local company, Western Electric, was a disaster before the employees could ever arrive at their destination. While waving goodbye from the decks of the SS Eastland, onlookers watched in horror as the ship leaned and then rolled over into the Chicago River. Screams of disbelief echoed through the city, and it appears that many lives have been lost, families drowned in the waters! I am miles away, but I see the image in my head, and I gasp for breath at the thought! When we made our journey on the SS Berlin, we feared death with every rocking motion, but we survived that trip across the ocean. Yet here, docked and smiling and anticipating a fun day, these innocent and hardworking people were doomed! What a sad, sad turn of events from peaceful waves and poetic lines to painful sights and devastation. I thank God my brothers are safe, and I pray for all those who died. In Jesus' name I pray. I promise to keep prayer in my life as long as I may live.

James paused.
"Should I continue?"
Dad nodded.

1916 To dream: Over a year in, and we are exhausted. All four of us have worked as laborers in several different areas: on railroads, in tunnels, as bricklayers. Angelo found extra hours at one of the meat packing companies, but his stomach couldn't take the stench, so that job didn't last. No matter what we do, we pool our money together in hopes of starting something of our own. Pietro now works for a construction crew, and he hears that new buildings are coming to Taylor Street and the blocks north and south of it. He wants to open a bakery, but no one else is excited. "It's what Mamma would want," he tells us, but we all know that Pietro is the only baker, the only one who took interest in baking with our mamma, so of course he would say that. We each have different passions. Paolo the artist, Angelo the musician. "What are we supposed to do? Open a gallery or a concert hall?" That is always Pietro's response, so I never bring up the idea of opening a print shop like the ones east of us. In Pietro's eyes, if a structure is built as a bakery, we should buy it. "It makes financial sense, and we might not all love baking like me, but we all know how to do it." I can't argue that point. Paolo challenges our eldest brother with, "What about Mamma's wish for us to make our dreams come true? A bakery is not my dream; it's yours." There is no discussion. Pietro has been talking with builders. I can only assume that it won't be long until we have enough money to buy something, and with Pietro taking the lead, it is sure to be Russo Bakery.

This morning I took a walk to the lake before sunrise. It was a dark and quiet and soothing stroll, and now I sit on the rocks, listening to the waves ebb and flow. I am reminded that I am a single speck in this universe, a single blessed speck in a world of mystery and delight. Whatever the future holds, my brothers and I are sure to do it together and stand united. I am glad that I took this moment to write, to breathe, to dream. The sun is creeping over the horizon, and my heart bursts with joy for no other reason than that I am alive and well.

"Vittorio is definitely a poet," James said.

"Wow. Dad, I guess you were right about the bookshop honoring the brothers."

"I didn't know how right I was when I made that statement." He took a deep breath and then turned to James. "I'm going to check on the oven. Anyone need something to drink?"

"Thank you. I'd love a glass of water, Mr.—Paulie."

When my dad left the room, I asked James to reread the previous entry in Italian.

"In Italian?"

"I just want to hear the way it was written, the way it was meant to be heard."

He smiled. "I like that."

The timer went off again.

"Last batch!" Dad called from the kitchen.

James reread the last few lines with the accent and beauty of its original language. I couldn't make it all out, but I caught the words "*sole*," "*cuore*," and "*gioia*." Each one sounded beautiful, and I smiled.

I noticed he was blushing after he paused and then asked, "What do you think?" he asked.

"I like that." There was a hint of flirtation in my voice and eyes. I caught it. I didn't mean to do it, but I recognized it. And I didn't hate myself for doing it. I didn't even offer a mental apology. James smiled at me and then looked up to my father to retrieve the glass of water.

"*Grazie*, Paolo."

This time my dad smiled and pointed to the folder.

"One more entry before I call Pompei about my dinner order."

1917   To support: We have much to look forward to, as it has been a busy year of change. We have a bakery on Taylor Street! It's a wonderful frame property with—

"Wait," Dad interrupted. "Did you say 'frame?' Not brick?"

"It says 'frame.' That's strange, right?"

"Hm. I'm sorry, James. Continue."

It's a wonderful frame property with a large three-bedroom apartment on the second floor. We all live upstairs, each of my brothers having a room, and I sleep in the living room. Animosity continues in our lives as Pietro brings his controlling leadership to the store, but we don't let him upset us. Just the other day, Pietro shouted to Paolo and me, "Why aren't the biscotti cooling yet?"—a question and a reprimand in the tone of Mamma when she asked who left their dirty dishes on the table. We could have explained that a customer cleared our shelves of cuccidati and pizzelle, and we thought it wise to replenish those goods before making more biscotti, of which we already had dozens packed in containers, but that would have fueled further shouting because Pietro thinks the bakery runs smoothly under his direction solely. Paolo was ready to retort, but he took a deep breath instead of making a comment about the biscotti recipes needing new flavors anyway. "They'll be cooling in ten minutes," I said. Pietro untied his apron from his waist and threw it to the ground, marching out of the kitchen in a huff. Angelo stepped out from behind the doorway and smiled at us. Paolo picked up a pizzella, freshly dusted in powdered sugar and blew a puff of air in Angelo's direction. We laughed at the childhood prank we used to play with pizzelle as Angelo brushed the sugar from his cheek. Pietro is so serious all the time, but he means well all the time, too.

Paolo met a German girl from Hull House a few blocks away. She is more reserved than the Italian girls we've grown to know and appreciate, but she is a good baker, having trained in the Hull House kitchens. Pietro is not happy about her relationship with Paolo, but he approves of her working for him as an apprentice. (I'm sure Anna—that's her name—thinks of herself as a lead baker, however.) Angelo got married just three months after we moved in. His wife Letizia lives with us, too, and she is a Godsend to our chaotic family. With Anna in the shop and Letizia in the home, we have all matured, and the bakery is thriving. I think Pietro is jealous of his younger brothers finding their wives because last month he announced that he is getting married, too. Her name is Francesca, and he will be moving in with her family near the corner of Milton and Oak. We met her only once. She is a quiet Sicilian girl, and I worry about Pietro's temper being a good match for Francesca's home with her father and a brother who is rumored to hang with a bad crowd. However, I do look forward to taking over Pietro's room.

Now, with three of the four of us settling down, my brothers bring available women to the shop to meet me. It is futile. I am emotionally content with my memories of Maddalena with the purest admiration, and with this family, I will never be alone. I can't imagine falling in love again, but if the day comes, I will know, and it will not be by coercion or coincidence. In the meantime, I promise to do whatever it takes to keep my family together.

James finished reading, but Dad's thoughtful expression made me think he stopped listening long before the silence.

"A frame house?" my dad asked again, a wrinkle in his forehead reinforcing his confusion.

"I don't understand that, either," I said.

The phone rang, and my father switched expressions after answering it and hearing that our food was ready.

"Can I change that from pick-up to delivery?" he asked.

"I can go," I said, but he put his finger over his lips to motion me to hush.

"Perfect. We'll see you in a few."

"Dad, it's not a problem for me to get the order."

"I know it's not a problem, Toni. But why leave? This gives us time for one more page before we eat. The next is 1918 and WWI must come into play."

1918   To be dutiful: We're in the midst of tense times. All four of us were required to sign up for the draft. I was the only one called to duty, and I am thankful. Pietro's wife Francesca was pregnant when we registered. Paolo and Anna married at the beginning of the year, and just before I left, Angelo and Letizia announced they were expecting, as well. With my brothers starting families of their own, I was living in daily worry for them. For me, I had only to pack a bag. I viewed training camp as a new adventure, and I understood the responsibility I was called to. My mind went back and forth like a teeter totter, first fearful and then excited and then fearful again. I was aware of the physical fitness drills, and I was correct about the grueling workouts. One thing I looked forward to was the English class to which all immigrant trainees were assigned. I learned more in the first month of training than I ever expected. The living quarters, however, were the most dreadful of the entire experience. We stayed in overcrowded tents in every phase of weather. Sickness was everywhere, so it was no surprise when I caught pneumonia. Luckily, I was too confused to remember the agony of my symptoms. I do recall, however, calling on Mamma for help and praying for a miracle, which I received: I was discharged and sent home to Chicago where Anna and Letizia nursed me back to health. For that I am eternally grateful. One day Francesca came to check on me, bringing along her "sick soup" stocked with healing herbs and vegetables. It tasted wonderful, and when I thanked her, I noticed the tears in her eyes. "Are you ok?" I asked, and she cried. She confided in me that Pietro had been more agitated and hotheaded than usual lately, that the Black Hand had extorted money from him twice, and she feared he would do something stupid in anger to provoke retaliation. It was the first time I heard of anyone dear to me being blackmailed, but all of us in the neighborhood know about them.

With all that has happened in 1918, the business surprisingly continues to do well. My prayer for 1919 is that we never go to war again and that the Black Hand leaves my family alone. I promised Francesca that I would remain dutiful to my family and protect them in every way possible.

"Prohibition and the mob are on their way to Little Italy," Dad said.

"I never knew about the Black Hand before Richie's story the other day," I told him. "Were they part of Capone's thugs?"

James explained, "The Mano Nera tortured their own Italian brothers through extortion letters, and they came through on their threats. When you asked me about the resemblance of the 'I' in Paolo's signature to an arrow, the dagger symbol was the first thing I thought of. Those letters that were written to the victims, they ended with deadly drawings on the bottom of the page. Skull and bones, daggers, black gloves. It was a scary group, but I think their organization ended when the Outfit took over."

The doorbell rang.

"I guess it's time to eat," Dad said as he walked to the front door.

"Should I stay or let the two of you digest this story along with your food?"

"My father would be offended if you left now. You are personally invited."

*   *   *

After dinner, we packed up the mostaccioli in airtight containers and stacked them on the kitchen counter. We decided to call it a night and reconvene on Saturday. It had been a long day. I walked James to his car and gave him a hug. He clung to me a bit longer than I expected.

"Call me when you and your dad are ready for my return."

"I will."

"You'll be sick of my voice before our next date," James announced with a grin.

"I can't imagine that happening," I said, and then I added, "When we're finished learning about the Russo brothers, I'd like the opportunity to learn about you, James."

"I don't have anything that will match the stories in that folder. Hope I'm not a disappointment."

"I can't imagine that."

*　*　*

I took out Mom's beads to start a rosary, but I honestly couldn't keep my eyes open. I fell asleep sometime between the first and second decades.

Saturday

A fresh base coat, sealed exposed brick, and refinished oak floors: anything was possible on this blank canvas. To create a reading corner based on Great Grandpa Paolo's painting was a captivating idea, and I imagined the grapevine design running through the entire space. Richie talked to the muralist who was enthusiastic about the project, and she scheduled a consultation for Monday. Richie also found a sample of textured tile that looked like flagstone to bring to the meeting. Richie stayed late into the night to finish the recessed lighting and hang antique pendant lights in the proposed reading corner. Everything was moving along.

I walked through the back door to find Dad tending the garden. The tomato vines were still bearing fruit, as were the cucumbers and Melrose peppers. It had been a good season for the peach trees, too. As I approached, the aroma of fresh herbs lingered in the air, and I thought, *"What an energizing smell!"*

"Good morning," I said.

"Ah, Mimma, it's good to see you this morning." He started to rise, dirt on the knees of his jeans, a trowel and pruning scissors in his gloved hands.

"Don't get up," I told him as he leaned over to kiss my cheek.

"Look at the basket. I'm done for the day out here." He went to the shed, opened the doors, and walked in, placing the tools in their assigned bins on the labeled shelves. He was a meticulous gardener. He was meticulous and organized with most things and never reprimanded me when I did not imitate that trait. "You're more like your mother," he used to say and chuckle at my lack of strategic instincts, "but we all get the job done." Which we did, even if that meant that Dad had to reorganize and reclean.

"Grab that bag of peaches, and I'll take these vegetables. I'll put on some coffee."

Upstairs, the fragrance of baked cookies lingered, but everything was tidy so that no one would have guessed that we had made a mess with baking ingredients and floured counters. He had packed away the treats before icing them, so he asked if I wanted to help.

"I will if you wait until this afternoon. A breakfast meeting is scheduled with my web designer. She's going to set up the bookstore online and sync the Point of Sale system to the checkout system on the site."

"I haven't the faintest idea what you just said, and I'm glad I don't understand it." Dad playfully covered his ears. The technological advancements had not been easy for him. Prior to the bookstore transition, he was still using the old cash register and handwritten receipts in the bakery downstairs. Even his clocks were read by numbered hands and the clicking of a seconds ticker. He used an old boombox to play his Italian music or lite rock, whichever he was feeling on any particular day, and that was the extent of his sound system.

He set down two cups of coffee. "Is James coming back with you this afternoon?"

"That's the plan. Is that ok?"

"I like him."

"I think I do, too. It's too soon to tell."

"Sometimes, it takes no time at all."

"Life isn't a Shakespearean play, Dad, and James and I are a far cry from Romeo and Juliet."

"Ah, but you can't deny that there's a spark, right? You recognized that spark in less than five days."

"What makes you say that?"

"When he was reading to you in Italian instead of English. I heard it in his voice, and I saw it in your eyes."

"Please, Dad. You're making something out of nothing."

"Maybe. Maybe not. Or maybe we fight things too much, put up walls and deny and think and analyze until the feeling passes." He stopped. "Don't do that, Toni. Don't fight against possibilities."

"I won't, Papà. I promise."

We took a few sips of coffee in silence, another thing I enjoyed about being with my father. We didn't have to talk all the time. All those mornings when he "read" the newspaper at the kitchen table while I sat across from him with my school books and notebooks, I remembered that his eyes were fixed, just staring at a page as if it was a prop for the drama inside his head. I didn't have the courage to ask him what he was thinking. Maybe I didn't want to know. Maybe I needed him to think I was studying for a test and not reliving all the imperfect ways I had treated my mom. Maybe our silence was what we needed back then because silence was safe while words created vulnerability. Too much mute existence could be detrimental, but over time, once we clawed our way through the pain and recovered from it to some degree, once we cleared away the magnolia's fallen leaves, when dialogue became more natural, we still took comfort in silence from time to time, as much as we took comfort in speaking.

I took another sip of coffee and asked, "What's on your agenda today?"

"I'll do more baking, maybe biscotti this time. I want a nice tray to drop off at the church."

"That sounds good. Save some for me, please, and then we can have Pompeii leftovers for lunch, right?" Dad gave a slight nod as he sipped his drink. "Let's say noon?"

"Perfect."

*　*　*

James and I pulled up at the same time. He greeted me with a single red rose. "Russo is a variant of the word red," he explained and gave me a kiss on the cheek.

"It's beautiful, James. Thank you." *Maybe Dad was right. Maybe this is a spark.*

Or maybe I'm just smitten.

Dad was also impressed. I didn't think he wanted anything more in life than to see me happy. At this moment, I was.

"You're as romantic as Vittorio," Dad pointed out. "Now let's hear what 1919 has in store for us, yes?"

"I'm ready," James replied.

We sat down in the same spots as the night before, and I opened the notepad, skimmed my details from the last entry, and wrote "1919" at the top of the next blank page.

"I'm ready, too," I said.

1919 To love my family: It is the end of December, and it is cold. Angelo and Letizia are living with me in the apartment along with their son Marco. Paolo and Anna are living next door with their son Antonio, and they are expecting again in early 1920. I wish the delights of parenthood were the same with Pietro. His story is difficult for me to write, but I will do my best.

After hearing about my brother's problems with the Black Hand, a new rumor was spreading that Francesca's brother was a part of that gang, probably giving information about Pietro in the first place. Angelo and Paolo and I discussed what we could do. We wanted him to move back to our home above the bakery, to bring Francesca and their baby Giovanni. But we all knew Pietro's pride, so I suggested we give him gifts to let him know how special he was to the brothers and then broach the topic of moving back to the family apartment as a gift in return to us. We asked him to stay after work for a family meeting. He stayed and was surprised by our thoughtfulness: I wrote him a short poem that Angelo put to music and that Paolo used as inspiration for a painting. "No matter the dreams destroyed, reborn; no matter the distance in time and place; home is in the mind and heart, a silent image of joy and peace." The tune had gentle picking, the way Angelo played to put little Marco to sleep or to quiet him during a tantrum. The painting was reminiscent of our home in Italy with stone paths and arched doorways, Calabrian grapevines weaving through the scene.

"Oh!" I gasped as I placed my hand over my mouth.

"The painting was for Pietro," Dad said out loud.

"Can you reread Vittorio's poetry?" I asked James. "I want to think of the painting while I hear this part."

James pointed to the place he left off and let his finger backtrack.

"No matter the dreams destroyed, reborn; no matter the distance in time and place; home is in the mind and heart, a silent image of joy and peace."

James paused, and Dad nodded to continue.

The tune had gentle picking, the way Angelo played to put little Marco to sleep or to quiet him during a tantrum. The painting was reminiscent of our home in Italy with stone paths and arched doorways, Calabrian grapevines weaving through the scene. "This is beautiful," Pietro told us. "A beautiful gift I am not worthy of." That's when I spoke up. I told him that I wanted him back home, at the family apartment above the bakery, that it would be such a help if Francesca could care for Marco and Antonio from time to time when Letizia and Anna were busy, that the three little Russo cousins could grow up like brothers the way we did. Pietro knew what we were doing. He thanked us for our concern, but he said he would handle his life on his own. That was his decision until a few days later when he went home to find Francesca with bruises on her cheek and neck, bruises given to her by her brother who was demanding a hundred dollars, money she did not have. Her father walked in on the assault and threw his son out, telling him never to step foot under his roof again, that his name from that day forward was Judas.

Life seemed calm for a short time after. Paolo's painting laid proudly on Pietro's dining table until he could bring it to the framer. Francesca healed quickly, but then Giovanni became ill. It was a Monday morning when Pietro checked on his tired wife and feverish baby after a sleepless night. "If there is no change by daybreak," Francesca whispered, "I'll send for the doctor." Pietro arrived at the bakery before sunrise as he always did, but I noticed his pale skin and shaky hands as he made the bread dough. It took some coaxing, but he finally revealed that he was worried about his son, that Giovanni was burning up all night. By mid-morning, there was still no word from his home, and after the last batch of rolls and cakes were in the ovens, I told my brother to check on his family.

A couple hours passed, and Pietro had not returned. Angelo and Paolo and I wanted to know what was happening, so we left Anna and Letizia in charge in order to head to Pietro's place a few blocks away. When we arrived, the undertaker's vehicle was parked in front of their building. Francesca was in a chair on the porch with bloodshot eyes staring out at the street. Pietro was punching the front door, bleeding knuckles and a bleeding head. We took hold of our frantic brother and held him until he collapsed into our arms, and through the sobs he cried out, "The Black Hand were in the living room when I arrived. They pushed me outside so that I could not enter my own flat!" Pietro wailed as he pushed us away, his hands burying his face. "They had Francesca locked inside, and they demanded a hundred-dollar payment." Between silence and tears, Pietro continued speaking of what had occurred just before we arrived. According to his details, he tried to reason with the Mano Nera, explaining that he did not have the cash and that his son needed a doctor. My brother fell silent again. I thought it best to bring the distraught parents inside, so I helped Francesca to her feet and guided her to their bedroom to rest, while Angelo and Paolo led Pietro by the elbows inside the home to the couch. I fetched a glass of water that Pietro refused. He tried to calm his breathing and went on with his story. "A burly man with a pistol reminded me of what happened at the corner last week, of the neighbors who did not come through on their payments, and paid with their lives instead." He let out a painful scream, "'My son is ill!' I told them over and over! 'My son is dying!' But they did not listen and demanded the money again. Oh, Giovanni!" My body was filled with rage as Pietro—my brother, Mamma's son, Francesca's husband, Giovanni's Papà—as Pietro said he tried to storm past the ruffian and got hit in the head with the butt of the man's gun. He was trying to get back up and go after the brute when he heard his wife. 'He's not breathing! He's not breathing!" Her crazed voice rang in his ears as another thug stepped onto the porch and told his crew that the baby was dead. "The cowards dispersed, and when I entered the room, my poor Francesca was holding my poor son. Limp." Pietro grabbed the water and threw it across the room as he shouted, "And no one came to help! I saw all the people peeking through their curtains, and no one stepped out!" I assured my brother that someone must have snuck out to get Dr. Caliendo who was there when we arrived and still outside with the caretaker. "No matter," he replied as he let his exhaustion take control of his body, as he slumped into the couch pillows. "Giovanni is gone."

James paused before continuing.

There was no calming Pietro. There was no calming Francesca. For days they only wept, and then the decision was made. Francesca and her father moved back to Sicily while Pietro moved in with me until we could get our family finances in order. He brought with him the clothes on his back and Paolo's painting. We had it framed and hung it on the wall. Pietro must have never looked at it after the day of Giovanni's death. If he had, he would have noticed the Black Hand's last signature, a dagger smudged onto Paolo's name. My heart is weeping.

Not a word was spoken for several minutes. Dad took a handkerchief from his pocket and dabbed at his eyes.

"My heart is weeping, too," he said.

I felt it. Even if Pietro and Francesca were relatives of the past, they were a part of us. When Dad turned on the television on the morning of September 11, 2001, his tears were unconsolable because he wanted to be in New York with his sister and cousin, because his family was in trouble, because that's what families do—they take care of one another, laugh and cry with one another, feel joy and pain with one another.

Too many times I felt that gut-wrenching sadness, in life and in literature, especially when I was a child and read *Bridge to Terabithia*. Maybe *The Diary of Anne Frank*, too. They were the stories that stayed with readers because we felt close to those characters, and when they experienced sorrow, so did the reader.

"Things have to get better," I said, partly as a statement and partly as a question.

"If you don't mind, I'm going to lie down for a short nap." Dad got up and started to walk down the hall. He stopped, turned back to shake James' hand and said, "I hope you're still up for joining us at the Feast tomorrow."

"I am, sir," James replied.

Dad patted his shoulder. "Good."

Before turning into his bedroom doorway, Dad said one more thing. "*Grazie*, Giacomo."

I agreed a break was a good idea. James needed to run some errands and asked me if I'd like to join him, but I declined. I walked him to the door.

"In the midst of all the pain of that last entry, I realize I still have a question about the painting," I mentioned.

"What's that?" James asked.

"I first thought the smudge was an arrow because it was pointing down toward the secret door. Why was it hanging there, directing my eyes to the floor?"

James was quiet for a moment, and then he said, "Maybe just a coincidence."

* * *

I searched for my rosary cheat sheet, the one that listed all the prayers and mysteries. I found it and scanned to see the mystery for the day. "Saturday. The Joyful Mysteries." Joyful was not the word to describe the last of Zio Vittorio's entries, but a thought raced through my mind. *It's not Russo Books.*

I texted James a question about an Italian word, and his response hit all the feels. "Thanks," I texted back. And with that, I prayed.

SUNDAY

The Feast of St. Anne, Mother of the Blessed Virgin Mary, was celebrated at the Church of the Holy Family. We celebrated the role of grandparents, too, as Anne was the grandmother of the baby Jesus. It was sure to be a great day of fun with games and food stands and music. Roosevelt Road was backed up for blocks, and parking was sparse, but when I finally arrived, Dad was at the bakery booth handing out his cookies to rave reviews. He enjoyed seeing smiles on the faces of those he served. This church was his blessing when he moved back into the neighborhood. He joined the mens club to keep busy and social while mourning my mother's passing. He rekindled old friendships and went bowling. His recipes were added to the parish cookbook, and he became an usher at the daily masses. Some people may underestimate the power of prayer and community, but not at Holy Family. This congregation was different, special. The church's history went back to the Great Chicago Fire of 1871 when flames threatened to burn it to the ground. The O'Leary family were parishioners, and it was behind their barn that the fire had started. When their pastor Fr. Damen was out of town, telegraphed news was shared with him about the nearby flames. He prayed to Our Lady of Perpetual Help to save the church he had started fifteen years before. He promised to light seven candles at the statue of the Blessed Mother when he returned.

From what I've read, the winds changed direction, away from the church. It survived. When neighbors took flight from the devastation, when they lost their homes and livelihoods, it was at Holy Family where they found shelter. It was at Holy Family where prayer and community flourished. At Holy Family, seven candles continued to be lit long after the flames died out, and the significance was more than a beautiful building being saved along with intricate wooden carvings and statues, stained-glass windows and bell towers. The significance was that people were saved, both physically and spiritually, within the confines of this holy place. Dad was saved here, too.

"Your friend is around here somewhere," Dad told me when I walked up to give him a hug.

"He's early, then."

"Late is bad. On time is good. Early is best," he reminded me, one of my father's bits of advice for living my best life.

"Well, well. Look who we have here," said Mr. Joe, approaching the table.

"Good to see you," said Dad.

"I'll take a plate of those mostaccioli, and a date to start those mandolin lessons," the old man stated.

Dad grinned as he handed the plate.

"I've been giving it some real thought, Mr. Joe, and I think I might just take you up on that."

"Really?" I asked excitedly.

"It would make Zio Angelo proud, right?"

Mr. Joe took a bite of a cookie and responded with crumbs coming out the sides of his mouth, "Feels like Christmas." He lifted a hand to say good-bye and was on his way to the next booth.

As the chimes rang the noon hour, James appeared at the table.

"I've been waiting for you. I didn't want to be rude and start eating without you."

"You didn't have to wait on Toni," Dad said while handing James a plate with two treats. I stole one while James took the other. One bite, and I was grinning from ear to ear. James closed his eyes as he chewed.

"Good, right?" I said, my mouth in mid chew.

James was more polite by finishing his mostaccioli before speaking.

"Wow, Paulie. Those are some delicious treats."

"We can thank my great grandmother."

"Want to walk around a bit?" I asked James.

"I'd love to."

We strolled down a path lined with magnolia trees, and I mentioned the mess they'd bring with the next rainfall.

"I'll take the mess if it means I get just one day of this fragrance and beauty."

We were headed towards the arts and crafts table when I felt his fingers brush mine.

"Do you mind if I hold your hand?"

I wanted to say that I didn't mind, truly, but I didn't say anything at all. The pause was too long.

"That's ok," he said. Instead, he gave my hand a kiss and released it. "Let's get some Italian ice," he said with a handsome grin. "Italian ice always makes me happy. You, too?"

I nodded. Vinny knew that those little pieces of sour lemon inside the smooth scoops of flavored ice were probably one of my favorite summer temptations. I nodded to James but didn't say anything again, even though I wanted to tell him, *Yes, James, that always makes me happy, too.*

* * *

It was late in the afternoon when we returned to Taylor Street. Dad and I took James on a walk-through of the bookstore progress, pointing out what had already changed and what was yet to come. It was the first time he saw, in person, my great grandpa Paolo's painting, and James especially liked the idea of bringing the image to life as a mural in the reading nook. All three of us were excited for project completion.

Even though we had been in the sun all day, the weather was uncharacteristically mild, so we decided to bring some glasses of iced tea to the backyard and relax on the patio. The yard was an oasis from the heat and crowds as the garden and flowers framed the lot. Dad took pride in this sanctuary.

"So, Giacomo, let's toast to translations." My father held up his glass, and we followed suit, clinking iced teas across the round, tiled table, leaning in under the green umbrella in the center.

"The next promise is dated 1920," James announced. "Should I begin?"

Dad nodded.

1920   To be thankful: There is no question that the German of the family takes charge of the Italian business, for Anna is the only one of us who knows Mamma's recipes. Pietro taught her well. Her dark hair matches ours, so on the rare occasion when she works in the front, no one thinks she is anything but Italian. Her light skin and blue eyes are the only giveaways to her real nationality, but that escapes most people because her speech is so fluent that no one knows Italian is her third language behind German and English. Paolo has done well by her, beautiful inside and out, and smart, so smart! The family embraces Anna, and she embraces all of us. Having been orphaned, Anna sees us as her only family, and that has become a blessing for the Russos. We brothers have commented that we feel Mamma's presence when Anna bakes. This past Christmas, she made trays and trays of our ancestral mostaccioli, so we could celebrate as we did in the Old Country. Even though it has been many years, I often wonder how Maddalena would have fit in in the bakery as Anna and Letizia have become quite the pair! There are times when I think they read each other's minds. When a child is crying, they don't ask one another to help. Whoever has hands free simply brushes them on her apron, walks out, and returns with one little boy on each hip. Two highchairs are set in the corner of the shop, and there's a treat on each tray all ready with a bottle and a toy. Angelo and Paolo come out to make the young boys laugh, and sometimes Angelo will play a song in the middle of the day when there's a line of customers. He says the music is for Marco and Antonio, but everyone knows better. He loves his mandolin, and the customers love it, too.

"There's your answer, Dad," I interjected.

"My answer?" he asked.

"You wondered if Zio Angelo would be proud of you for taking mandolin lessons, and there's your answer! He would love it!"

My dad nodded and pointed to the instrument across the room. "You can go on, James."

It was time for Pietro to join his wife Francesca in Italy. He left before the holidays, so he gave me his Christmas gift early. When at the train station, we hugged and kissed each other on the cheeks. He pulled back with tears in his eyes and then reached into his coat pocket. "I have something from Mamma," he told me. "These are her beads. She gave them to me in Calabria and instructed me to pray on them and think of her. I have done so, but I want them to be passed down to one of the boys. Antonio or Marco, you can decide when the time is right." Mamma's rosary. I remembered her nightly routine of kneeling in front of a statue of the Blessed Mother, a wooden figure whittled by her brother and blessed by our local priest. Her hunched posture was my last image every evening before going to bed. Holding her beads and letting them wrap through my fingers, I promised to pray on them until the day comes to hand them to another Russo. I miss Pietro, with all his gruff and controlling ways, and all his brotherly love. I pray every night that Mamma is protecting him. I pray for his safety and peace. I pray for his happiness.

James paused. No one had told him to stop, so he went on.

1921 To share: I remember the deep purple skins of the gaglioppo grapes that lined the fields on the other side of town. I remember working in those vineyards and taking breaks to snack on the fruit's sweet flesh with the juices trickling down my lips like a sloppy child. I remember Maddalena standing beside me and using her apron to wipe my face clean. When I smile at my dearest in gratitude, she reminds me that someday she'll be wiping the gaglioppo wine from lips in the same way. During these Prohibition days, this memory often enters my thoughts.

We have a loyal customer named Al. He is a local businessman who helps run a neighborhood soup kitchen, and although there's been talk of a connection to the mob, he has shown nothing but kindness to us and our community. One day when the ladies were upstairs putting the kids down for a nap, I took over the counter, serving whoever came through the door. When the bell rang, I came from the back and greeted Al. He noticed right away that there was a blue mark on my palm. "Are you mashing some grapes, Vittorio?" he asked. I brushed this off with a friendly response. "And if I were, I wouldn't take you as the undercover type." Al commented, "If I had a badge, I'd wear it proudly. There would be no undercover for me, my brother. I only ask because I'd buy a secret bottle right now if you had something to share." Prohibition has become a challenge for many people. I did have a bottle. We make our own wine, just for the family. Not to sell. But Al has been good to me. I trust him.

"Anyone else a little worried about Vittorio's friend Al?" I asked.

"It feels cordial. Maybe it's not what you're thinking," James said. "Maybe his last name is Marino or Romano instead of Capone?"

"I think it's Capone," Dad replied.

"We'll find out soon enough. Here's another one from 1921."

1921   To be a friend: I am conflicted about Al. Last week he needed a special delivery of cookie trays, but at the last minute on a Sunday. He said he would pay well. At first, I said the money was not the point, but he insisted on making a lavish payment because he knew Sundays were precious family times. I don't know what it is about him, but this is not the first inconvenient request, and I succumb to him because he has a special charm that I deem friendly. He returns favors for me, too. He is financially generous to our business and community. But his insistence in paying me makes me feel like I'm being bought, and that is not true friendship. I ponder what to do.

The bakery continues to do well, so we are in a position to close on Sundays to keep our spirits alive. After church, we picnic in the backyard, and when the children rest in the afternoon and their moms prepare for the family dinner, the ladies keep the door and windows open to hear Angelo's mandolin. Paolo sketches, and I write. The experience lasts only an hour or two, this one time every week, but it's enough to fill our hearts. I remember only the habits of working in the bakery every day, and I rarely recall the sermon of Sunday masses, but the real memories and the holiness of our existence come when the Russo brothers inhale Calabria and exhale Chicago, breathing steadily and joyfully. Dinner is always followed by storytelling and laughter, a sip of homemade wine, a nighttime prayer, and grateful tired eyes. I am blessed.

"That's a beautiful image," I thought out loud.

"Beautiful, yes, but I get a feeling that something is on the horizon here," James said. "The calm before the storm."

"Like Richie said about the Black Hand. Very few families of Taylor Street could have escaped a Capone connection, and no relationship with Al could be kept without joining the outfit. I pray that that's not the direction this is going," Dad worried. He stood. "I need a glass of water. Do we want some dinner before we continue?"

"I have to admit that I glanced at the first line of 1923, and personally, I'm eager to find out what happens."

"What does it say?" I asked.

"There was a fire."

Dad sat down again. "We will eat and drink after 1923."

1923 To trust: There was a fire. We lost much but not our lives. There was an investigation. The fire marshal determined that the source of origin came from an unattended coal stove. It was a controlled fire, but the damage to the bakery made all contents unsalvageable, and the smoke destruction made the upper apartment uninhabitable. The finger was pointed at Anna, but that, in my opinion, is impossible. I was with Anna when closing the shop. She, of all people, is the most responsible member of the bakery and family. I do not know how this came to be, but it was Al who came to our rescue. Associated with demolition services and construction companies, knowing about insurance and city codes, our friend led the renovations for us. Paolo and Anna remained in the apartment next door. Angelo and Letizia went to live with Paolo's family, as did I, sleeping in a makeshift room by putting a mattress in the pantry, but I didn't complain. "How could we ever repay you?" I asked Al on the day we returned to our new business and apartment. "If tables were turned, I know you'd do the same for me, my brother." That's what he said, and it was true. I still believe he is a good person, no matter the rumors that continue to be whispered on the street.

The new building is made of brick, a brown, tan color like that of a cup of coffee with a dash of cream. The bay window isn't straight anymore, but three-sided with more display options for the passersby. All the kitchen equipment is updated. We could never have afforded such appliances and pans and utensils. Although Anna and Letizia were apprehensive, they can't hide the excitement. They are baking and serving in a shop they could only dream about. They are the envy of all the women who work along Taylor Street.

Al renovated our living space with new furniture and clothes. Paolo and Anna were leery. Angelo questioned the overabundance of gifts. "How much do we pay him?" asked Angelo. I replied, "He says we owe him nothing. He says that someday down the road, he might be down on his luck and need a friend, and that's when we will be there." I am not naive. I am simply optimistic.

If business had been doing well before the fire, nothing prepared us for the business that started coming through the door after the remodel. We had to hire more bakers and delivery staff. With the new storage shed in the backyard, we are able to house extra equipment and ingredients we never had room for. The shed floor is covered in pallets to keep products off the ground, and shelves are built into the walls. Al was sure to advise us to keep our accessories and containers on the shelves in case of flooding in the back. A smart idea. He is always stopping by and giving us tips on what we should and shouldn't do, and I am fine with the suggestions because they all make business sense, and he is a top business man. My worry is that Al seems to talk like a Russo Bakery partner, which he is not. I wish Pietro were here. I wrote to tell him of the situation, and he advises to take precaution when it comes to Al. He and Francesca are doing fine. That's *what he says, but there are no details on what "fine" means to him. I continue to pray.*

"So the brick building we now know was built in 1923 with the help of Al Capone?" I asked.

"Do we really believe it's him?" James added.

"That can't be good," said my father.

"I'll keep reading," James concluded.

1924 To teach: Buon Natale! I have so many festive memories from growing up in the Old Country; however, this past Christmas was such a delight as we started making special memories with the next generation. Our living arrangements remain the same with Paolo's family next door and Angelo's family in the apartment with me. On Christmas Eve, the children walked around the flat looking for the statue of baby Jesus, and once it was found, they sang songs of the season, all in Italian. Anna made a feast beyond our dreams. We thought we had sold out of the zeppole, but Letizia had boxed up two dozen! The children's smiles of awe on Christmas morning made everyone remember what this day was all about, and we prayed and cried. This was not about gift giving, but being together and bringing joy to family, joy to the world.

With time off from school, the children play up and down the block with all the neighborhood kids, and the sound of their laughter is contagious. They have snowball fights and build snow forts along the sidewalks. So different from Calabria, but beautiful. With soggy boots and iced mittens, the children run into the bakery looking for cookies, and Letizia yells at them to go out and come back in like civil children. They do so, ask politely for cookies, and Letizia smiles and gives them each a treat. Without ever having met our mamma, Letizia has her childrearing ways. I still hear Mamma's voice telling us boys that respect in the house shows respect for God. "Rispetto!" she yells in my dreams, pointing a rolling pin in our direction, and when we respond "Sì, Mamma," she opens her arms wide to collect us into a family hug.

Since Antonio and Marco started school, academic problems have been apparent. The boys don't speak much English because they are surrounded by the Italian language and culture every day. Rarely does anyone speak English in Little Italy. Anna came to me one evening and made a special request. "Can we count on you to help the children with their studies?" she asked. "Education is very important to me, Vittorio, but I can only do so much between the business and the family. I need your assistance as the only other person in the family who can speak the language of their school teachers." I agreed, of course. My nephews are like my own, like the boys Maddalena and I never had, and I'd never say no to Anna. (I think she had known that before she asked for my help.) From that moment forward, when the boys come home from school, they come straight up to the apartment and sit down at the kitchen table. We read together and write out the alphabet together. We add apples and subtract cannoli. Ha! To Paolo's amusement, we draw pictures, and the boys' artwork is always better than mine. I thank God every day for my family, and especially for this new generation sitting beside me.

"I like the picture in my head," I said

"It's a happy moment," said Dad, but his facial expression did not show happiness. When forehead creases deepened, I knew thoughts of worry brewed.

"What are you thinking about, Dad?" I asked, no longer the teen lacking the courage to ask that question.

"My parents moved me away from the Italian neighborhood, and I missed out on the language and culture. Even though I was a second-generation Italian-American, it seemed like I was the first. My dad grew up in Little Italy, which was removed in many ways from American culture, even when living in the city. As much as he missed his daily life in Chicago, maybe he agreed more with my mom than I originally had thought. Maybe he didn't want me growing up with the same academic issues. I don't know anymore." He sighed. "I think I want to end things there."

"How many more entries, James?"

"Only two: 1925 and 1929."

"What do you think, Dad? Should we finish this up today or tomorrow."

"Tomorrow."

"As you wish." I closed my notepad and returned it to the cabinet.

We decided on a morning meeting, and James said he could be back by nine.

* * *

Later that night, as I started my new bedtime routine, I paused before praying. I looked closely at the wooden beads draped between my fingers. *Could this be the same rosary that Pietro gave to Vittorio? Did Vittorio choose Antonio, and did Antonio choose my mom, his daughter-in-law?* I kissed the Crucifix and talked with my mom. And then I began my prayers, not needing the cheat sheet, mostly.

Monday

It was nearly 8am when I pulled up to the shop. Before getting out of my car, I texted Claire that I needed to reschedule my appointment. *"Sorry for the late notice, but I have some family matters to tend to this morning. Is it possible to reschedule for tomorrow at 10?"* She responded immediately. *"No worries, Toni. I'm available at 10. I hope everything is ok. I will see you then."* I grabbed my purse and checked one more time that I put my velvet pouch inside. I had. As I swung the car door shut, I looked up at the terracotta decor and smiled.

Dad was at the kitchen sink washing the few dishes he used for breakfast. A small pan was still on the stove with pepper and egg remnants and the smell of fresh garlic.

"Good morning, Toni. I'm just cleaning up," he said, placing his dish in the drying rack and wiping his hands on the towel. "If you're hungry, I could make another omelet for you."

"No, thanks, Dad."

He gave me a hug and kiss and went back to cleaning, scraping the leftover food pieces into the garbage can and placing the pan in the soapy water. After wiping the surface, front and back, three times, I giggled as he rinsed and moved the pan to rest beside the plate in the rack. "I think you missed a spot," I joked.

"Cleanliness is next to godliness," he replied, another of his favorite sayings.

As Dad brought out two coffee mugs and filled each, I took the pouch out of my bag and put it on the table.

"What's that?" he asked.

"Mom's rosary," I said as I slowly pulled out the beads, small, smooth spheres linked with tiny metal hoops and joined together by a two-sided medal with the image of Jesus and His Blessed Mother on the reverse. Dad reached out and took from my palm the Crucifix at the tail of the chain and lifted it to eye level.

"I haven't seen this in years."

"Pietro gave Vittorio their mamma's rosary, instructing him to pass it down. I'm wondering if he could have chosen your dad Antonio, and—"

"—and my dad could have given it to my wife?" He finished my question.

"Is that possible?"

"What's more possible is that my dad would have given it to Josie, and when it was clear to her that she wouldn't be having kids of her own, she gave it to your mom to pass on to you."

"Not you? Her own brother?"

"When it comes to our faith, Mimma, maybe I'm a church kind of guy, but your mom was the prayer lady, believing everyone was in need of a novena." He let the beads gather in his hand and folded his fingers around them before continuing. "And like I've said so many times before about the friendship between Amelia and Josie and Cousin Maria, they were closer sisters than any blood relation could be."

Little Women. It must have been the summer between first and second grade when Aunt Josie and Cousin Maria gave me the rocking chair. It sat in the corner of the bakery, golden oak spindles on the back, securing the headrest that had a painted scene of Little Bo Peep. I was still exploring picture books at the time, so Mom and Josie and Maria all took turns sharing the pages out loud, pulling up an adult chair while I rocked and rocked, listening to chapter after chapter as I met the March sisters and imagined being one of them. Years later, remembering the characters and some of the scenes, I picked up the book in the school library to read it, myself. I loved it all over again. I never gave appreciation to the first version of the story, though, the one

I had heard as a child, but I guess that's what we do sometimes, go through life without thanks until those little things come back to us and fill us with gratitude.

*   *   *

1925   To be vigilant: My optimism no longer exists. I've been too good to Al, not wanting to admit that he takes advantage of me, but now I know he is a no-good crook! A short while ago there was a raid on our building, and as I think back on that night, my heart feels as if it will pound right out of my chest!

It was late. We heard loud banging and yelling at our front door, and both Angelo and I bolted through our bedroom doors to see who was calling with such urgency. The officers wanted to know who owned the bakery. We said that we did, and we were handcuffed and brought to the jailhouse for questioning. Where was Al? When did he come and go? Did we know he had weapons and alcohol in our shop? We had to have known. Where was Al? Where were we hiding him? The honest truth was that we did not know.

Angelo and Letizia insisted on moving. I don't blame them. "Not far. Just down Bishop a few blocks." Now, I have the whole flat to myself, and there are times when I am scared. I sleep with a baseball bat under my bed. Yesterday morning when I entered the bakery kitchen earlier than usual, I found Anna cleaning the floor on her hands and knees. "I cleaned that last night when I closed," I told her. "And I clean it again before you return in the morning," she answered matter-of-factly. "You don't know that they drink and smoke here from time to time?" I didn't. I truly didn't. I asked Anna what she thought we should do. "We clean." That is her answer because Anna does not want Al to win. He may have built the structure, but she is the one who built the business. She is going nowhere, and I admire her so much. That night, I woke from a crazy dream and went to get a glass of water from the kitchen. Out back I saw the light of a match and a cigarette. Two men moved across the yard to the shed and walked in. I never saw them walk out. I waited a couple hours before sleep won the war on spying. Today I examined the shed, the pallet floor, and I remembered Al's suggestion to keep everything off the ground. I lifted the pallet and realized why it was important that nothing heavy sat on top of it. Underneath is a trap door! My heart is pumping hard! There is no way I want to find what that door leads to. The less I know the better. I just wish that Anna knew less, too.

"Zio Vittorio, how long did you keep these secrets? Til death?" Dad was taken aback by these new details, but he had become curious, too. He stood up from the table and walked toward the back door. Turning to us, he called, "Am I the only one who wants to check this out?"

James and I immediately hustled to the shed as my dad detached the hook and eye latch. We removed old boxes of garden tools from the flooring that was made out of rotted wood pallets, and then we pulled out the pallets to reveal the ground beneath. The trap door was visible. Completely visible. *All these years later, and no one realized what was under a few wooden boards!* This time the mysterious door had a handle, and it opened! James and I watched as Dad lifted the square entry, the hinges creaking, but there was nothing to see, no staircase, just a hole in the ground.

"Do we have flashlights?" James asked.

I hurried into the shop and grabbed three lights from Richie's tool supply. We all lit up the hole, and we confirmed there was nothing but four walls. Three cement, and one brick, the bricked-up wall facing north, directly on point with the bricked up wall from inside the bookstore tunnel.

A three-foot step ladder laid on a shed shelf, and James had the idea to lower it into the hole to investigate.

James laid down on his stomach and was able to feed the ladder to the ground below, but it dropped from his hands and fell over.

"It's deep, Toni. Should I go first?"

"I'd like to go first," I said. For some reason, I thought it should be family to discover whatever was down there, whatever Vittorio didn't want to know. Maybe something, or maybe nothing, no matter.

"Are you okay with lowering yourself in?" James asked.

"Of course."

"Be careful," Dad warned, a bit overprotective for a short drop. I patted him on the shoulder and smiled.

James got up, and I laid down on the ground, extending my feet into the hole and then inching my way back until my legs were dangling in the darkness.

"Be careful how you land so that you don't twist an ankle on the ladder down there," James instructed.

Already in an awkward position, half above and half below the earth, I turned my head to James and laughed. "I'm not sure how I'm supposed to avoid landing on the ladder, but I'll try."

With that I said, "Here goes," and dropped myself into the hole, landing on the ladder, and falling against the brick wall.

"Are you all right?" Dad and James questioned simultaneously.

"I'm good."

I used the flashlight to look around. Surrounded by cobwebs on the walls and bugs on the dirt ground, the space couldn't have been more than a five-foot square. No markings or treasures were left behind there, and the brick wall had the same reddish color as the tunnel's brick wall. "They were probably closed off at the same time," I called up.

"If there's nothing to see, then get yourself back up here," Dad said.

"I'm on my way," I answered, setting up the ladder, stepping up, and allowing James to help hoist me back into the shed.

"Well, that explains that." Dad got up, and James helped him close the trap door and replace the pallet. We returned to the kitchen.

"Anticlimactic or expected?" asked James.

"Both," said my father.

"We don't have much more to go with Vittorio's story," I reminded, brushing off the dirt from legs and arms. "How about we finish that last entry?"

"Absolutely," said Dad.

Just as James was lifting the folder, Dad placed his hand on the cover to prevent it from opening. "*Grazie*, Giacomo. You have been very helpful."

"*Prego. È stato un onore.*" Dad gave him the puzzled look again, so James translated. "You're welcome. It's been an honor."

Dad tapped James's hand, and then he motioned to open the folder.

1929   To be moral: I do not want to put our family in harm's way, so I remain silent about the tunnel, about Al's meetings in the bakery in the middle of the night. Anna remains silent, too. Al never asked for anything from us, until the end of January. He sent word to me that he was having a package delivered to the shop, and he needed me to deliver it to him at his home. The package arrived, and I took it to Al who insisted on opening the box in front of me. Police uniforms. "Ever wonder what it would be like to be a cop?" he asked. "Not at all," I told him. "Humor me, Vittorio. Try it on," he instructed, holding a blue shirt in his left hand, a policeman's hat in his right. I replied that I would not do that. Al chuckled and then said I had been a good friend, so he'd let me continue to wear an apron instead of a badge. That he'd let me wear an apron? I know better than to have too much pride and ego, Pietro's characteristics but not mine. I smiled and was escorted out, never to hear from Al again.

On February 14, the newspapers proclaimed the massacre that Al orchestrated with his thugs dressed in police uniforms. It was too much for my heart to take. I told my brothers and their wives. Anna and I have revealed the secret passageway, and it's a relief to have shared that information. Paolo says the tunnel won't be used while Al is in Florida or in jail, but he worries that our home could be raided again. Angelo insists on hiding his cherished mandolin and all our treasures. "We need to protect our most prized possessions," he announced. I still sleep with a baseball bat at my side, but my mind is clear.

"So, Vittorio was unwilling to help Capone," my Dad said.

"He used his conscience. That's a big deal, Dad."

"It *is* a big deal. I think I have more pride in being a Russo than ever before."

James lifted the last entry page and noticed a pocket on the back folder flap. He slid his hand in the opening and pulled out an index card.

"There's one more."

1947   To make no promise: I recall the poem "Promises Like Pie-Crust." As a baker and as a man, I know the analogy of brokenness all too well. Instead of making promises, I long ago decided simply to live a good life and have been doing so all these years. I want Mamma and Maddalena to be proud of the mark I leave on this world. I think I'm doing all right.

I am the only Russo brother left. City workers are coming to brick up the tunnel. Part of me wants to bring our treasures out of the darkness before that happens. Another part of me thinks buried treasures are a reminder that we can't live in the past. It is time to look to our future, to the next generations of Russos. I'm not sure how our story will unfold, but I look forward to turning the page.

* * *

"I'm gonna give it a go, Mom," I said out loud while folding up my cheat sheet and putting it in my drawer. With my hands holding the silver cross, I closed my eyes. *Zio Vittorio. I am so grateful for these beads, and I, too, promise to keep the family prayers alive.* I took a deep breath and began, "In the name of the Father, and of the Son, and of the Holy Spirit. Amen."

TUESDAY

Early Tuesday morning, I stopped by the shop to talk with Richie. The muralist had met with him yesterday. "She can't wait to get started," he told me. I brought him out back to the shed and showed him the latest discovery, an escape route exit, and I explained that there was nothing but four walls inside.

"Damn, Toni. Had a feeling there was some kind of Outfit connection to the tunnel, but I never heard any rumors or old stories about this place," he said, "and I pride myself on knowing the rumors." He laughed at himself.

I told him we had ancestors who never wanted the Russo name to be associated with Capone. I left him to work on the flagstone tiles and then met my father upstairs.

*   *   *

To my delight, Dad was in the living room picking strings on the mandolin.

"So, you're going to take up Mr. Joe's offer of lessons?" I asked.

"Yes. I am," he replied confidently.

"Good for you!"

He rested the mandolin on the couch and then came to me to place a kiss on my cheek and tousle my hair.

"I have to say that even though these 'promises' were hard to hear at times, I find the whole experience fascinating, don't you?"

"I do," Dad said as he led me towards the kitchen.

"Do you think Zio Vittorio lost his joy after all that happened to him and his brothers?" I asked.

"Maybe," Dad answered, setting down our mugs of coffee. "I do think he probably lost sleep every night of his long life, though. That's not joy."

"*Gioia*," I said.

"That's 'joy' in Italian, right?"

"Yes. That's what I want to call the shop."

Dad stopped mid-sip. He paused in thought.

"Toni, that's perfect."

"The bookstore fulfills all the promises. To write, to dream, to teach. Everything. The beauty of it all could be our generation's way of bringing joy back to the family."

I saw the tears coming to his eyes when he replied, "That's beautiful, Mimma."

"I'm thinking we could host a monthly tribute to 'joy' with local author readings, folk music performances, and artist displays."

"A monthly tribute to joy," he repeated. "And we could serve Italian cookies and wine?"

"Exactly."

"*Gioia*. It's perfect."

*　*　*

I arrived a few minutes early to my 10am appointment with Claire.

"So, tell me about your week," she said, an innocent and loaded statement.

"What do you think about magnolia trees?" I questioned.

"I never gave them much thought. Why do you ask?"

"I don't give credit to a magnolia's beauty and fragrance while it's in bloom. I need to focus on that."

"Really?"

"It was a good week," I declared, and then I went on detailing each day's events.

* * *

It had been a hot day, but as dusk arrived, it was a bit cooler by the lake with a sky turning to a sea of lavender and orange hues. James and I sat upon the rocks along the shore of Lake Michigan, listening to the waves ebb and flow.

"I wonder if this was the spot where Vittorio came to think and write," I thought out loud.

"Wouldn't that be something," James replied, a grin forming at the possibility.

I felt the hard, smooth stones beneath me, relishing the image of Vittorio, and then I asked, "Do you remember when I asked you for the Italian translation for 'joy'?"

"*Gioia.* Yes," James replied.

"That's going to be the name of the shop. *Gioia,*" I announced.

A smile appeared from ear to ear. "I love the name, Toni! When did you think of that?"

"This might sound silly, but I've been praying the rosary, and when I said the Joyful Mysteries on Saturday, the idea hit me."

James touched my back, briefly. "I don't think that's silly at all," he said, leaning in.

"Yesterday confirmed it for me. I realized that this bookstore is all about bringing joy to my family, to this community, to me."

"I think it's brilliant."

He raised a store-bought latte to toast the idea, and I touched my decaf lid to his. We drank, and then I laughed. "Do you think we drink too much coffee?"

"Ha! Can you believe it's only been a week since we had our first cup of joe? That feels impossible," said James.

"To be exact, this is our ninth day of knowing each other."

"Ninth? Were you saying a Novena for me?"

His question puzzled me.

"You're not the only one who grew up with a rosary, Toni. Novenas are prayed for nine days."

Mom? Are you here? How did this happen?

After a brief pause, something dawned on me. "I never gave a direct answer to your question when we first met," I said.

"What question did I ask?"

"You asked if I believe in coincidence, and without thinking I said 'no' and then I thought about it and said I wasn't sure and then I said I didn't want to think about it."

"I remember the question now."

"No."

"No, what?"

"I don't believe in coincidence. Might not understand everything that happens in life, but when I reflect back on events, I can see who I become after the incidents take place. It was not a coincidence that I met you, James. And for the first time in a long time, I'm happy." I took his hand and held it.

"You know what I'm feeling right now, right?"

At the same time, we both said, "*Gioia.*"

When we were heading away, I told James I needed to stop at the shop to pick up my bag, my old school bag that now carried my bookstore notepads, tape measure, flashlight, paint chips and wood chips, and more miscellaneous items I never thought I'd ever own let alone keep with me at all times. James pulled up in front of the building and asked if he should go in. I told him only if I'm not back in five minutes; it means I've stumbled down another rabbit hole. As was my new habit, I stepped out of his car and looked up at the terracotta blocks that outlined the rooftop. *I promise to be observant.*

As I opened the door, the bell's tinny sound whispered at my entrance, and I flipped on the light switch. The illumination wouldn't have revealed much to a stranger, but to me, a whole world shone bright. Memories of display cases and the smell of fresh baked goods appeared before me and then faded into a future view of reading nooks and rows of books with the aroma of coffee beans and almond-like scents of pages worn and new.

My heart was full as I imagined the day Vinny and I sat in the exact spot where I now stood, discussing the dream over espressos and biscotti. *I miss you, Vinny. I'll never let go of your love. I'm just letting go of the sadness.* I picked up my bag from the corner, the place where my great grandfather's painting would soon come to life. *I'm happy, Vinny. I promise.*

The door's bell rang again behind me, and I heard James say quietly, "It's just me." I wasn't startled at all because I knew it was him, just like the first day we met.

* * *

Before taking out my rosary beads, I said a prayer to Mom. *Thanks for the novena.*

Six Months Later

I touched the velvet pouch in my pocket before stepping to the center of the reading nook, Great Grandpa Paolo's artwork restored and hanging behind me. Dad was picking his last chords on the mandolin as the crowd listened attentively while snacking on biscotti and espresso. I stood in deep awe of the fruits of our labor. A thunderous round of applause exploded when Papà stood and took a bow. He leaned in to kiss me on the cheek and whispered, "I'm so proud of you, Mimma. It's your time to shine."

There was no microphone. It was just me and a piece of paper with thirty to forty sets of eyes on me. Family and friends, neighborhood business owners, former colleagues, old classmates, local book enthusiasts.

"My script says that I should start with a poem, but honestly, looking out at you all, I'm so overwhelmed with gratitude that I have to begin with that. Richie, I almost didn't recognize you without your torn jeans, work boots, and ripped t-shirts." Laughter lifted the air. "This renovation was all *you*, my friend. Through every discovery, uncovery, and recovery, you were there to breathe life into a vision, and I am grateful for you."

I took a pause to raise my cup in Richie's direction, to allow him the recognition he deserved.

"Papà, there are no words. Only you and I know the journey we've been on. Together, we've learned about our proud past, together we celebrate our present blessings, and I look forward to embracing the future that awaits us. *Ti amo.*"

Another burst of applause rang out.

"As many of you know, Russo Bakery was a staple in Little Italy for decades. The support our family has received for generations is appreciated more than you'll ever know, and it is my hope and prayer that your support will continue as we open our doors to this space. A bookstore, yes, but so much more. A place we can gather as a community to honor the old days and explore the new, through literature as well as music and art. What an inspiring room this will become!"

I took a sip of water before finishing.

"This bookstore is a tribute to four immigrant brothers, who, a century after their arrival, talked to me in ways I never understood before this venture. In a sense, this bookstore is a dream come true for all of us." Reality set in. I needed to pause to keep my composure, and then said, "The following poem was written by my ancestor, Zio Vittorio, after arriving in Chicago in 1915. It's been translated by my dearest, James."

I mouthed "*grazie*" and smiled when he mouthed back "*prego.*"

She comes to me at night
in my city dreams
sitting on a stoop on a hill of homes
shared with sisters and brothers.
So poor in pocket, so rich in heart!
She comes to me at night
bouncing a baby boy on her knee,
her finger in his mouth
taking on pain to relieve him of his.
She comes to me at night
with netted hair and apron,
flour embedded in the nails
of strong hands, ready to fulfill
the family needs.
She comes to me at night

too frail to breathe
and yet she inhales for me
and exhales for you,
her soul so ready to go,
but first—
first we must promise
To dream
To laugh
To pray.
So we pack our bags, and we're on our way.
Four lonesome sons, her blessed boys,
Who always remember they're Mamma's joy.

ACKNOWLEDGEMENTS

There are so many people to thank in this endeavor! I am grateful for every family member and friend, student and colleague who has supported me on my writing journey, as well as the readers who have followed me on social media. You inspire me to keep at it!

I especially want to thank all those who were road trip companions in the summer of 2023. When I had to meet a first draft deadline but didn't want to forgo the mini-vacations, you all had my back and gave me time and space to do my thing, encouraging me the entire time. I adore you, my dear cousins, my college girls, my grade school friends, and my sons. Oh, those sons of mine! Ethan and Liam, you are my heart and soul, and I thank you for being YOU and for believing in ME.

Thank you to Christopher Whisperings, an amazing new publishing company, that has guided me with patience and professionalism. A highly recommended writing experience for all those who have a manuscript or are currently working on one.

This novella has been a labor of love, inspired by a passion for my ancestry, for all things Chicago, and for writing. I hope you enjoyed the story!

Nonno Antonio, you are forever in my heart! And Mom, I'm glad to know I read the dedication to you before your passing. I will continue to find joy in our memories.

Also by Geralyn Hesslau Magrady:
  Lines (2015)

Follow Geralyn Hesslau Magrady on
   Facebook.com/writer.GHesslauMagrady
Book Group Questions and Ideas Available at
   www.ChristopherWhisperings.com
Teacher Resources and Classroom Discussion Prompts Available at
   www.ChristopherWhisperings.com

www.ingramcontent.com/pod-product-compliance
Lightning Source LLC
Chambersburg PA
CBHW060506300726
48975CB00008B/2674